NOMED
"SOVEREIGN REIGN "

Timothy Middleton

DEDICATION

This book is dedicated to the people who enjoy vampires just as much as I do.

ACKNOWLEDGMENTs

I would like to thank all of the people that believed in my dreams and aspirations. I hope you enjoy reading this book just as much as I enjoyed writing it and developing its characters. I hope that you enjoy the characters. I wanted to give you my view of the characters so that you could see them as you go on this amazing journey. I would like to thank Michael Toney for bringing my characters to life out of the descriptions I gave him. I am truly happy on how they turned out.

chapter 1

"Tilt of Power"

In 2000 BC, there stood Dracula, a man sent to walk the world in darkness for choosing to smite God when asked by the creator to walk and share his vision with the people of the world. Since Dracula was cursed by God for eternity, he found a way to create people in his own image to walk the darkness with him. Dracula, after countless trials and test, found out that by a human drinking his blood or being bitten by him, he could turn humans into the walking dead like himself.

Over time, these people became known as vampires. The first three vampires to be created were Norie, Raven, and Bones; who he tasked to go out and spread his world of darkness to the humans of the world. These new vampires found out fast that they had an uncontrollable need for blood. Similar to that of a child surviving on milk, they drank blood of humans as much as they wanted. These vampires, along with Dracula, came to be known as the Bloodlust Four, spreading terror through the world for ages. Like Dracula, eventually they learned how to not kill as many humans in order to survive, along with how to use the dark powers that were gifted to them through Dracula's blood.

Norie

Dracula gave each vampire a piece of land to rule over the and to build his empire. Norie was given a captain position over the house of Dracula (which located currently in the America's region) since he was the first vampire to be created. Norie came to be known as the reaper by those who have faced him due to his ability of blood manipulation. Norie is able to take the blood out of any person's body he has killed and use it to create anything he imagined; whether it be weapons, buildings, or even blood like humans . He always carries around a capsule on his back filled with blood so that he is never without any at any given time. Rumor has it that he leveled and entire battle field of humans with a gigantic blade that continued to get bigger as the more people he cleaved in two. Despite the intimidating abilities Norie possesses, he was still considered the weakest of the initial three vampires Dracula created.

Bones

Bones was given the house Koben (which is currently located in Afracian region) Bones' powers have been said to terrify even the gods. Bones has the ability of body manipulation. Bones can make any dead corpse come to life and serve Bones until his dying breath, no matter how weak or strong the corpse is. It has been said that he could raise the bones of the dead to do his bidding as long as he killed the host while it was living which led to Bones being given the name "Undertaker".

In the house of Koben, there is said to be a variety of extinct animals and beast that protect the vampires of the house of Koben, including two of the strongest elder werewolves that were eradicated from the face of the Earth by the vampires. These werewolves are specifically responsible for protecting Bones. No thief, soldier, or opposer has ever made it out of the house of Koben .

Raven

Raven was given the house of Talos (which is currently located in Eurasia). Raven is by far the strongest of all the original vampires created. Raven has shotgun like powers. He has the power to point out any spot on a person's body and instantly make it explode, which was why he was given the name "Deathscream". The bodies of his victims are never in one piece because he decides to blow multiple holes in them. Even though he has super strength and could easily topple the strongest of vampires, he finds joy in having the view of body parts flying in the air as he tortures his victims.

The Fall Of Dracula

Just how Dracula created three vampires, he also created three noble families: The Horens, Viridan, and Stratfields to protect them while they sleep during the day. Due to Dracula seeing an increase in humans' will to fight against vampires, each noble house was given prized vampires with extraordinary abilities to protect them and essentially look over them to make sure they are staying in line.

These families have kept the balance between vampire and humans for ages now. They know all the dirty secrets of the families and the vampire houses, and the noble families keep up the checks and balances between the two races constantly at war. Nothing goes on in the world without them knowing about it.

The truth is the noble families have been studying and looking for a way to take control back from the vampires but they could never find a way to kill them. Using the sunlight would not work because the main parts of the vampire houses were underground and remained constantly protected. One thing that the families know is that Dracula usually moves alone because he believes that no one can touch him since he is the strongest person on the planet. The nobles' have a scientist that has been translating scrolls and writings that they have been secretly stealing from the vampire houses for decades now and finally they found out the location of where Dracula was changed by God into a vampire.

The rebirth of Dracula was in the middle of an island in the Bermuda Triangle, so instantly the three families convened and decided to go search the island for clues. The families sent their brightest scientist to the island. When they got there, they realized it was nothing but a big hole with strange writing all over it. They immediately started to take pictures of everything and immediately streamed it to the families.

As the scientist searched the hole, they run across a door. They opened it, shining their lights down the dark gloomy doorway and walked in. Immediately, the door shuts behind them and lights come on. Unknowingly, they had mistakenly walked into Dracula's home away from home and all the families can hear and see are yells and images of blood everywhere coming from the group of scientists they sent. The last person alive grabs the camera and yells, "Please help me. He is killing everyone!" He is quickly pulled into the darkness thereafter. After killing all the scientists, Dracula walks up and looks in the camera and tells them he will find them and he will kill them. He vows that no one will ever know about this place. In his head, he has no idea who sent the scientists, due to the fact they had no seals on their clothes.

With all the scientists being killed, the noble families rush to have everything returned by the time Dracula makes it back to the house by night fall. As the sun goes down, Dracula appears in front of Norie and asks, "Have any humans been in the house?" Norie replies, "No! There has not been anyone in your house!" Dracula goes to his library next to make sure all of his notes are in place. He sees that everything is where it should be, so in his mind, he assumes it was a random accident of how humans found his home. Dracula then proceeds to each noble house to question them about how he was found while he was out sleeping. All of the families said they did not have any clue on how he was found. Secretly, they had already begun to decipher the markings on the walls of Dracula's birthplace.

The next day, the three noble houses met during the day to read what they had found from the data. One key fact that they found was that Dracula has an incantation that puts him under control of whoever speaks the incantation to him; as long as the wielder has the blood of the vampire he speaks the incantation to. Upon learning this, the families realized that they had the key to stop Dracula because they already had his blood on file. They sent a message to have Dracula come see them as soon as night fell.

They patiently waited for nightfall and as soon as Dracula arrived, he immediately felt the air in the room was wrong. As he prepared to disappear he heard *"Alon tatarus demon!"* He was instantly frozen like a statute. Remaining still, his anger shook the entire room as this great black shadow expanded and then went back into Dracula's body. As the nobles walked up to him, they made him tell them everything about the Bloodlust Four and how to control all vampires. Then, after they took all the information they wanted, they told him to go to sleep until they asked him to awake. Then they hid him away so that no vampire would ever be able to find him for eternity.

With Dracula gone they easily took over the other vampire houses and used incantations to make their leaders act as they commanded. This is how humans took the power away. The noble families now controlled Dracula and made vampires their slaves and weapons. The families now use there prized vampires to hunt down humans or vampires that get out of line from what the nobles are trying to create.

The Noble Families

The Stratfield's

The Stratfield's are currently led by Dr. Montague, who is now commander of the Afracian region. Little is known about him, other than he has a fondness for unique vampires. Just like all the other houses, Dr. Montague has had three vampires under his control that were passed down to him from his father and their fathers before. Their names are Braden, Calderon, and Turan. Braden is one of the strongest telepathic and telekinetic wielding vampires in the world. Calderon is an elemental vampire who can make anything that is of earth, wind, fire, or water become whatever he imagines. Turan is a master of pyrokinesis. He can produce flames and create beings out of fire to serve him in and aid him in battle.

DR. MONTAGUE

The Viridan's

The Viridan's are led by Mr. Beaumont who has been the commander over Eurasia region for the last fifty years. He fancies in having the strongest vampires out of his region to serve him. Their names are Leo, Demetri, and Arnoldo. Leo, who from his time of being turned has studied swordsmanship, is known as the number one ranked swordsman in all of the land. He has never been seen without some kind of knife with him. He usually carries multiple swords on him at all times.

Demetri is a natural fighter. He has mastered every type of hand to hand combat known to man. His only downfall is that once he starts fighting, he cannot stop until everyone is killed and the room is covered in blood. Arnoldo is a vampire of brute strength. He is able to move mountains if he so wishes.

MR. BEAUMONT

The Horens

The Americans region is ran by the Horens and is stationed currently in the United States. Their leader is Ms. Gladstone. She is said to have the youngest, but strongest three vampires under her control from the house of Dracula. Shelby, who is known to be able to create a shield, has the ability to cover fifteen people in a bubble. Inside that bubble they can have secret conversations, be protected from harm or danger, and she can even let vampires walk in the sun for fifteen minutes before the shield runs out. There is no one that Shelby has known that is able to penetrate her shield. Second is Gillie, who is a time shifter. He can move forward and backwards through time for short periods, however, depending on how grave the period of time he is moving, he will temporarily lose his powers. Gillie's powers can sometimes have dangerous consequences. Lastly is Nomed, who has not been around as long as the others before him. He came to the house of the Horens 500 years after the disappearance of Dracula. Although Nomed has only had a short time here in the house of the Horens, he has certainly made his mark thus far.

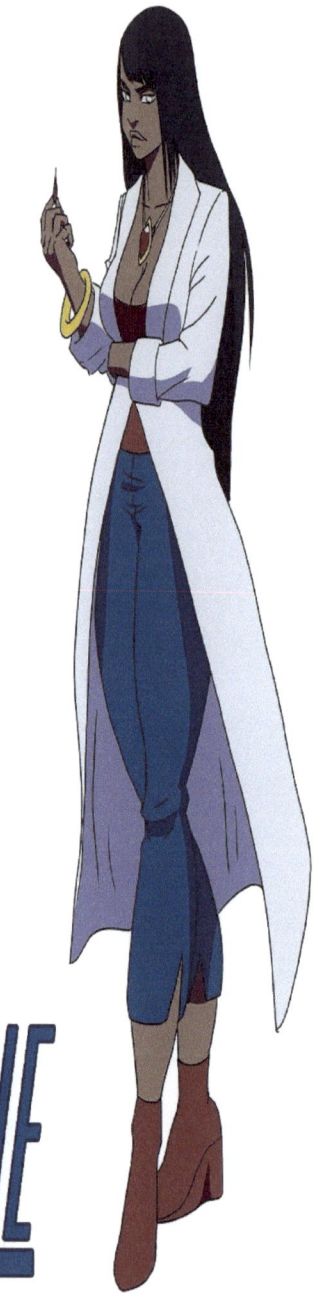

MS.GLADSTONE

SHELBY

CHAPTER 2
"Nomed"

All anyone knows is that Nomed has multiple powers but nobody knows the limits of those powers. In fact, Nomed does not even remember where he came from or when he was first created. All that he does know is that whenever he sleeps, he feels this instant surge of uncontrollable power flowing through him. He has no family other than Gillie and Shelby. No one had any idea who Nomed was, but they accepted Nomed as family just as Mrs. Gladstone did. Even the eldest of vampires had never seen Nomed before. They said he popped up out of nowhere so in turn they have treated him as an outcast.

When the eldest vampires talk about Nomed, you can tell they have even treated humans with more respect than Nomed. Because of this, he has always seemed to feel unsure on who to turn to about how to get answers on who he is and where he comes from. Despite treating Nomed like an outcast, they also fear Nomed due to the fact he has no vulnerabilities like all other vampires, other than sunlight. In his countless battles, he has never been severely injured and the more he gets beat up the stronger he becomes. One thing that Nomed has noticed is that certain vampires that he kills, he gains their power. It doesn't happen all the time, but selectively, he gains the abilities of those he has defeated. For that exact reason, the Horens vampires have been tasked with defeating all vampires that are deemed deadly by the noble families.

Present Day

Nomed has been a loyal servant to the Horens for years; with no real ending in sight for him. He has been called upon to be considered a weapon until the end of time, and even being used having to hunt down and kill his own brethren on occasion. No matter how corrupt or evil a vampire is, it still hurts to have to eliminate a brother in arms and it pains Nomed to have to endure that. The noble family has never understood that vampires are not like the ones that are perceived in the movies – loving, easy-going, and understood. They are vicious, malicious, and in many ways, like caged animals trying to hold back this insatiable urge to feed on their prey. The noble families have tried to help with the killing of humans by giving out free nectar (synthetic blood) to all vampires to save from the bloodshed of humans, but it is said those who drink human blood can never truly go back to only drinking nectar. The eldest vampires are the only ones allowed to hunt humans to feed but even they are still monitored closely.

Suddenly, Nomed is brought out of his deep thoughts as Mrs. Gladstone walks up to him and demands that he go to the meeting room. As he walks in the room, Nomed can feel the air is stale and the look on Gillie and Shelby's face tells him that something is wrong. As he walks deeper into the room, Shelby puts a shield over the three of them in order for them to talk in peace. Shortly afterwards, Mrs. Gladstone walks in and tells them the Horens have been requested by the Viridans to kill Demetri because they cannot control him when he goes on missions. She goes on to say that Demetri just kills everyone in sight; even women and children. After hearing the news, the Horens team of vampires are all against killing a dear friend they have worked with for years, but regardless of how they feel they will be forced to complete the mission or someone else will. While Mrs. Gladstone continues to talk, Nomed, Gillie, and Shelby are devising a plan to save Demetri while they are still protected in the shield.

They finally come to the conclusion to record a fake death of Demetri when the time comes around to fix the problem. They then hear Mrs. Gladstone yell, "Do you understand that this mission must be done and do you accept?!" Unanimously, everyone agrees and the team is given the location of Demetri. He is located in the Ural Mountains, a place known for its heatwaves that cripple normal humans.

As Nomed and the team enters the plane and prepare to find Demetri, he begins to think back on the times where him and Demetri sat down and talked about how he couldn't help himself while killing people and how he never understood why he could not control himself like other vampires. The entire plane ride was filled with various memories and conversations that Nomed and Demetri had over the years. All of a sudden, they hear over the intercom that there are five minutes until they are over the drop zone. Gillie looks around and realizes that there are no parachutes on the plane.

"How are we supposed to get out of the plane?" he asked.

"I have an idea," Nomed says, "Shelby can create a shield that will catch us when we fall."

"And what if it doesn't catch us, smart guy?" Gillie said. He wasn't convinced at all that this plan would work.

"Then we will break a few bones, heal up for a few hours and then start hunting," Nomed said.

As they all walk to the end of the plane, Shelby puts a shield around them and they all jump. As they plummet towards the ground, everyone's eyes get bigger as they see the ground getting closer and closer. When they hit the ground and as the smoke clears, all you can see is a cracked shield disappear. All three of them get up and begin to laugh saying, "I can't believe that worked!"

As they began to look around, it was clear that it would not be hard to find Demetri. All they had to do was follow the piles of dead animals and bones left in his path. The pile led them to a cave deep in the mountains. As they walked in, they lock eyes with Demetri.

Demetri

When Demetri finally sees who is in his cave, he says, "So they sent you to kill me." As fast as lightning, Demetri rushes them. Nomed dodges and looks back as Demetri's punch explodes and a hole is in the wall.

Nomed yells, "Your fight is with me and only me." Shelby begins to record their fight as planned. Demetri begins to punch Nomed repeatedly as he just dodges the punches, making Demetri's rage worse.

Demetri yells, "Why don't you fight like a man; you are doing all of this running instead of standing tall in the face of despair!"

Nomed replies, "It's not my fault you are not fast enough to catch me! In what age did people just let others hit them?"

As he finishes that statement, he dashes towards Demetri and punches him in the gut. Demetri's body lifts up slightly from the floor. While Nomed is caught off guard, Demetri grabs Nomed's hand.

"That's what I was waiting for. You finally got close enough," as he smashes Nomed across the face. If it wasn't for Demetri holding so tight to Nomed's arm Nomed's body would have flown across the room. As blood splashes out of Nomed's mouth, he looks up and kicks Demetri in his side. Demetri's body almost doubles over from the pain and he releases Nomed's arm. As Nomed swings his arm around, he begins yelling and taunting that Demetri has quite a strong grip for a girl.

Demetri stumbles back and stretches his back at the same time and says, "This coming from a fairy? Man I really should consider this an insult." Demetri then pulls a flask out of his pocket, takes a big gulp and throws it towards Nomed who catches it.

Nomed attempts to take a drink and says, "Hey it's nothing in here."

Demetri says, "I know. I don't share my liquor with kids."

Nomed notices that Demetri is right in front of him and says, "You've gotten faster…"

Before he finishes that statement Demetri begins to hit him with punches from every angle. Nomed begins to dodge them, but at the same time has to watch out for Demetri's grapple techniques, which is so powerful it can break bones.

Nomed says, "I won't let you grab me again. I am not going to fall for that again, but you are still too slow."

Nomed dashes to the right and starts to hit Demetri with quick jabs all over his body.

Gillie and Shelby are looking on and Gillie leans over to Shelby and says, "Doesn't it look like Demetri is having a seizure the way he is being hit?"

Gillie laughs, "I know I shouldn't laugh but it does look funny."

Shelby looks over and says, "You are such a child! I need you to focus. Our time could come any second now."

They both hear a big boom as they look back to the fight. Nomed has slammed Demetri into the floor. Demetri, as Nomed is pulling his body up, leg locks Nomed's arm and breaks his wrist.

Demetri looks up and realizes Nomed didn't react when his wrist broke. Just then, he sees Nomed's other fist coming down towards him. Demetri's body instinctively lets go of Nomed's arm and moves. As he jumps away, he sees Nomed's blow creates a crater ten times the size of the one from his body imprint. Nomed rises and looks at his wrist which has healed and he is moving it around. He looks at Demetri with a smirk on his face.

"Your body moved on its own, Demetri. It could tell that I was aiming to kill you. I see now that I can't play with you here. I thought you were just a strong drunk, but you're really a fully functioning drinker. I've never known someone who focuses in after drinking and becomes more of a tactical killer. I'm surprised you even changed fighting styles four times during our exchange of blows."

Demetri laughs and says, "I see you aren't a kid at all. You have bathed in battle in order to see the little changes of a battle like that, so I guess it's time I stop playing as well."

Nomed hears a voice in his head that says, "Let me kill him, let me help."

Nomed yells over to Shelby and Gillie, "I've got this you guys, stay out of the way!"

They both look at each other and say, "We never said we wanted to help. He is all yours."

Demetri throws a large boulder he found lying around and yells, "You need to focus on the battle in front of you."

Nomed looks at him and says, "You have my full attention. I'll give you that honor and end this fight in three minutes."

Demetri charges in and starts kicking and punching. Nomed is dancing all around his movements again and says, "I thought you were getting serious. I guess I'll show you the real difference in our power."

Finally, Nomed stops dodging and takes all of the blows head on and the blood begins to flow from Nomed's face. Demetri says, "This is you showing me your power? You are nothing but a weakling." Nomed just begins to laugh as his eyes turn black and the entire mountain begins to shake. As Demetri charges at him, prepared for another blow to Nomed's head, Nomed stops his punch. The wind behind it blows a hole through the mountain. Nomed smirks and begins to pummel Demetri and as Demetri begins to lose consciousness, Nomed breaks Demetri's wrist. The pain immediately triggers him back into consciousness.

Nomed then looks him in his eyes and says, "This is the level between us," as he rips off Demetri's head and holds its up for the camera to see. Immediately, Shelby shuts off the recorder and Gillie uses his time shifting abilities to erase the last fifteen seconds of the fight and resumes where Nomed stops Demetri's attack. Gillie and Shelby yell at Nomed to stop before he kills Demetri again simply due to the fact Gillie can only set time back by fifteen seconds once every three days; so if Nomed was to kill him again it would be permanent.

Luckily, Nomed does not have the same killer mentality as Demetri, or this plan wouldn't have worked at all. As the fighting stops they enlighten Demetri about their plans and notify him that they will have to lock him up in their secret base until they can decide what to do with him knowing they cannot let him run free. Because of his pure bloodlust and need to fight, they know their deception will be found out in no time due to his lust for fighting, so they locked him in their facility in Canada.

After they secured Demetri, Shelby says, "Good thing we bought this place a long time ago or else we would have had to really kill him. It's not like Demetri can blend in in normal society without fighting someone or something."
Nomed looks at Shelby and says, "That is a fact. He is a social misfit, but now that he is safely locked up, let's go before they wonder where we are."

As they returned to the Horens house, they were welcomed with high praise and were told their video was viewed around all the noble and vampire houses to show that there will be zero tolerance for rouge vampires.

A Blaze of Fire

As Turan returns from his mission protecting one of the Stratfield's nephews, they both walk into the safe house and see the footage of the fight between Demetri and Nomed. As he sits and watches, he tells everyone it's no way in hell Demetri loses this fight. Turan sees the events turn as he notices that Demetri is out classed he says to himself, *"I knew Nomed was strong but he has gotten stronger since we all last seen each other."* Turan continues to watch and as he sees Nomed behead Demetri, he drops everything in his hands and falls to his knees. Turan had created Demetri and upon seeing his son killed, tears begin to flow from his eyes. His screams of disbelief fill the entire room immediately.

Turan is overcome with anger and rage and in an instant he levels the entire block in a rage of fire, killing everyone that got caught in the blast. Turan, still on his knees finally comes back to reality as he smells the scent of something burning. As he opens his eyes, he sees that he burned an entire block of buildings and everyone in them. He can't believe his eyes. Right beside him is the Stratfield's nephew body. As Turan reaches out to touch it, the body becomes dust and floats in the air.

Knowing that he could not return to the Stratfield's house after what he has done, he fleas to his birth place in Africa, a city known as The Kalahari. To many, Kalahari is still considered a lost city that no one knows has been rebuilt. Turan single handily built the city back up as a safe haven for vampires who had lost their way or couldn't be around humans. As Turan entered the city, his friends rushed to let him know that he must hide because Dr. Montague already has Braden and Calderon searching the area to see if he had come back home or not. They rush him to a hidden passage of the city that is currently still being rebuilt. Little does Turan know, Braden had already felt him return to the city and he breaks away and goes to where he felt Turan last.

As Braden sees Turan, they both freeze and stare into each other's face. Turan then starts to throw fireballs at Braden, but he dodges them. As he dodges and moves in closer, he halts all of

Turan's movements as if he was being grabbed by a giant hand. When Braden is face to face with Turan, he simply laughs and says, "You really thought I came here to bring you back after all the missions we have been on?!" Braden expresses the pain of losing someone you created and how it's equivalent to a human losing a child. No matter how rude, unruly, and crazy that person is, they will always be someone who you love and care for.

He lets Turan know the truth that their leader Dr. Montague destroyed every vampire he ever created fearing that they could possibly become as powerful as Braden. "So when it comes to you, a person I've been with for so many years, I see you as my son. I want you to live no matter what you have done." He lets Turan's body go. With them both having a clear view of whose side each of them is on, Braden tells him just to stay hidden and don't draw any attention to himself until they can find out what to do with him.

As Braden and Calderon's team pushes out, he warns Turan that they will send Nomed after him after they return to Dr. Montague with nothing to show and without a body in hand. Braden embraces Turan and says, "You be safe my brother. If anything happens to you I will be saddened," and he walks away saying that you and Calderon are truly a handful. As the red sun sets Turan sits looking at a horse made of flames dance in his hand as he thinks about the impending battle between friends.

Turan Must Be Found

Nomed receives a text from Ms. Gladstone asking him to come to her office. As he proceeds to walk to her, he thinks it is about her finding out that they really didn't kill Demetri. Nomed opens the door and walks into the room. Mrs. Gladstone tells him to sit down and politely asks if he needs anything. Nomed thinks to himself, *"Why is she being so nice? She has to know something."* Then he replies no and takes a seat. Upon sitting down, Nomed is given a folder with the whereabouts of Turan. Nomed inquires why she handed him this and she says that he must be eliminated. Nomed then says couldn't you find someone else to do this job? Why does my team have to keep killing their friends just to make humans happy? Ms. Gladstone then recites the incantation *"alon tatarus demon"* and in no time, Nomed is on the ground in pain. Nomed could hear several screeching noises in the back of his head. He also began to lose his sight.

As she walks over to him she yells, "You don't think you are merely a weapon for me to use at my disposal? You don't want to be on my bad side! It wouldn't be wise for you to question me again!" She then releases the incantation.

All the noise going off in Nomed's head stops and he can finally begin to see clearly again. As he gets up to his chair, sweating as if he had just ran across the world, Ms. Gladstone says she would like to have this done as soon as possible. Nomed gets up and walks out of the office and goes to meet his team. As he walks into the room, he slams down the folder breaking the table in two.

Gillie and Shelby look at him and ask what's wrong. He begins to tell them what once again is asked of them. Gillie just laughs and says, "We will do the same thing from before then; it's no big deal, Nomed." What they don't realize is that the more they kill their friends the more the actual vampire race hates them, because the videos of their missions are plastered all over the television for the world to see. Nomed is upset because at the end of the day, there is nothing they can do about it as long as the nobles have control over them.

As the team gets ready to go to Kalahari to find Turan, there's no laughing, no games and no fun. The team feels like slaves going to go fake to the world that they are killing one of their friends. This time on the plane, there are six other military personnel there to film the death of Turan. While on the plane, Shelby creates a shield for her, Gillie and Nomed. Inside the shield, they are discussing how to get rid of the others without making it seem like they did it on purpose. Shelby devises a plan on how to get rid of the soldiers so that they can "get rid" of Turan on their own.

As they walk to the tail of the plane the six troops jump out with their parachutes. After they jump, Shelby covers Gillie and Nomed with her shield. On the way down, they pass one of the troops and as he gets close enough she envelopes his parachute. As they hit the ground, they eliminate one of the soldiers, and as the team gathers back together, they check in and let Ms. Gladstone know they have landed and are headed into the city. The entire walk, Shelby has up a shield and they are talking about how they can get all of the soldiers out of the way. They devise a plan to get the soldiers to try to flank Turan at his current position, but it will really be the main entrance to his hide out. By doing so, they will have no choice but to fight him and they will lose.

As the group walks into the city, they find nobody there. It almost looks like a ghost town. Nomed can sense where Turan is by the smell of smoke that always runs off of Turan's body. He immediately tells the soldiers to run to the deepest corner of the city to flank Turan and they will go to the other side to meet him head on. As the soldiers are walking through a corridor, they end up walking into a completely new city and right in front of them is Turan. In an instant, the entire squadron of soldiers are engulfed in a blaze of fire. Meanwhile, Nomed and the others are standing behind him just watching and erupting in laughter when they realize that with Turan eliminating the soldiers, their plan had worked out better than they'd hoped.

Nomed tells Shelby to put up a shield and to record the fight along with telling Gillie to make sure after he kills Turan to change back time. As Turan turns and see's Nomed he hurdles a massive fireball at Nomed and it is a direct hit. Nomed screams in pain and falls down after the fireball hits him. Turan walks over through the flames laughing.

"I thought the infamous 'Nomed' would be more of a match for me" he says as he walks over and pulls Nomed off the ground by his head, "Now, you will pay for what you did to Demetri!"

Turan then punches Nomed in the face, but Nomed's face does not move. Nomed opens his eyes after the punch and says, "Is that the hardest you can punch?" Turan has a brief second of fear because he does not understand how Nomed is not hurt from the flames. As he tries to piece everything together, Nomed uppercuts him towards the ceiling. As Turan's body is floating towards the ceiling he says to himself, *"Man, I didn't expect his punches to be so overwhelming."* He opens his eyes and sees the ceiling. Turan flips, braces himself against the wall and uses flames to throw himself off of the wall.

At the same time, he sees Nomed burst out of the flames headed straight towards him. Turan creates a giant fire fist as he and Nomed swing at the same time. The clash creates a blast that blows both of them into two different directions. Nomed gets up and brushes himself off. Turan is still struggling to get up as Nomed dashes over towards him. Turan begins to throw hundreds of fire balls at Nomed who doesn't dodge them. As they all hit his body, his sprint begins to slow down and as he comes to an halt, Nomed falls to the ground.

Turan says, "I knew you weren't that strong; I don't even know why I panicked. I thought you might be unbeatable, but it seems those flames finally caught up to you." As he picks Nomed up again, he continues to taunt him. "You are nothing but a candle in my flame, destined to burn out."
At that moment, Nomed's eyes open and his arm goes through Turan's chest. As Turan looks at Nomed in shock, Nomed whispers, "You are a weakling dancing with a God."

Shelby tells Gillie that she has the footage that they need and he can change back time. Gillie goes back to the time where the soldiers just burned to death. Nomed starts the battle from the beginning, telling them to stay out of the fight and that he must teach Turan a lesson but he will not kill him. Turan turns around and sees them and once again hurdles a gigantic fireball at them.

As it hits Nomed, he begins to laugh and says, "Is this all you got Turan? This could never possibly harm me." Nomed grabs the end of the fireball and throws it back at Turan. As Turan tries to catch it, Nomed comes through the fireball and kicks him into a wall.

Meanwhile, Gillie and Shelby are in their usual spectator roles.
"Shelby, did you know Nomed was fireproof?" Gillie asks.
"No, I had no idea, but what I do know is that Nomed is pissed about Turan's snide comments about him being no match for him," Shelby said.

As she finished her statement, Turan has a surprised look on his face as he pulls himself out of the wall, leaving an indention behind. He can hear Nomed in the background yelling, "Is that all that you have for me? You are pathetic!"

Turan, in a rage creates a whip made of fire and throws it at Nomed. He catches around Nomed's neck and propels himself towards Nomed. In Turan's other hand, he creates a blade of fire and rams it through Nomed. Turan, feeling accomplished and thinking he has won this battle, looks up only to see a smirk on Nomed's face. Then, Nomed breaks Turan's arm and leg with ease.

Turan screams out in pain and Nomed looks at him and says, "Now you know why my name is whispered around the world with terror."

He double clutches his fist as he jumps in the air and comes down across Turan's face, breaking the ground below both of them.

Gillie walks up and says to Nomed, "Did you have to be so harsh with him? Your pride is on another level, man. Just look at him, his whole body is limp! Are you sure you didn't kill him?!"

Nomed brushes by Gillie to pick Turan up and gets Gillie to help him carry all of the soldiers' bodies as well. They hide Turan among the soldiers' bodies that they are taking back with them. On the way home they stop by their facility in Canada and as they walk in, Demetri is sitting there. He looks up and sees Nomed, Shelby and Gillie.

"About time you guys come and visit me," Demetri says.
Shelby replies, "At least we brought you a roommate back." They place Turan's body in front of him.
"I knew he wouldn't go down easy, but did you really have to break his Turan's neck Nomed?" Demetri asked in between his laughter. Demetri placed his hands over Turan and begins to speed up his healing process. As Demetri's hands start to glow, you can hear Turan's bones snapping back together. As Turan wakes up, he looks at Demetri and says, "I thought that hell would be hotter and uglier than this," and then he begins to look around and sees Nomed,

Shelby, and Gillie. He immediately ask what's going on. Everyone begins to explain what has been going on and how now Turan must stay here in order to keep them from getting in trouble. They assured Turan that they will be able to run free when the time comes.

Turan states to Nomed that he misjudged his character and that he is one of the noblest vampires he knows and he is glad to call him his brother. He told him that he is forever indebted to him. When it is time to leave, everyone says their goodbyes and head back to the Horens house to deliver the video to Ms. Gladstone. When they arrive home, they show her the video footage of Nomed's fight with Turan. As soon as she sees it, she immediately sends it out for everyone in the world to see. Nomed and the team walk out of the room and into their sleeping quarters. As soon as they lay down, Ms. Gladstone yells over the speaker that there would be a meeting with the vampire houses and all the prized vampires immediately following sunset. They wonder what would could possibly be happening next.

CHAPTER 3
"The Meeting"

As instructed, Ms. Gladstone and the team walk into the plane to travel for the meeting that was called. They are met there by Norie and his first and second in command, a pair of twins called "The Night Riders", but their given names are Mario and Maurice, from house Dracula.

As they stare down Nomed with the nastiest of looks, Nomed snaps back at them, "Do I look like your maker or do I need to smash my boot across your face?"

Mario replies, "I have no problem killing a traitor." Just as quickly as he finishes that statement, Nomed has him by his throat. Shelby has his brother in a shield. As Nomed says he will snap Mario in two, Norie clears his throat and tells Nomed to look at his side and as he looks down there is a sword made out of blood ready to pierce his side.

Gillie steps forward and Ms. Gladstone finally steps in and says, "Alrighty kids, let's all play nice before I make this a painful ride for the lot of you."

With that threat being made, Nomed releases Mario and says, "Maybe some other time." Norie brushes by both of them and ask Ms. Gladstone where is the meeting going to be held. She tells them it will be in Atlantis, and that they should be there shortly. As the tension is still in the air, Maurice looks at Shelby and says, "Do you think Nomed will always be around to protect you from getting hurt? Don't think I forgot your part in this either, with your little shield."

Lights start flashing on the plane as they have arrived at their destination, Atlantis. As they look out the window, they land on this island with one big tree on it. Everyone gets off the plane and follows Ms. Gladstone to the tree and magically it opens. There is a giant room with a massive table that seems to be made out of the tree itself in the room with several chairs.

As Nomed looks at this table, he can tell that many important matters have been discussed on it due to the fact it is heavily marked by holes, scratches, and fist indentions. Ms. Gladstone tells them their section is at the top of the table. No one else had gotten there yet so they just take their seats. As everyone sits down, Shelby puts a shield around the three of them, so they can discuss things discreetly. As they are waiting, they are all trying to figure out why this meeting was called.

Finally, the secret door opens and in walks Dr. Montague followed by Bones and the first and second in charge; which are two beast-like humans that have red lighting erupting from their bodies. Behind them are Braden and Calderon. As they all lock eyes, Braden reaches towards the tree and breaks a piece off with his mind power and throws it toward Nomed. Before Nomed, Shelby, or Gillie could react, they are hit by a gust of wind. One of the beasts moved so fast in their direction that he caught the piece of tree and crushed it, and all they saw was him swiftly move back to the side of Dr. Montague.

As Dr. Montague looks at Braden he says, "You know better than to move without me giving you permission. Don't you let it happen again. We are here in peace and no one should fight in this room." He clears his throat and yells, "Hello Ms. Gladstone! It's been a while since I've seen you in person. It's good to see you. Nomed interrupts them and asks, "What are those beasts anyway?"
Dr. Montague replies, "Those are Bones' slave werewolves. They were all eradicated way before your time."
"Then how are they standing here?" Nomed inquires.
Bones walks forward and says, "Because I can control anything that I kill and resurrect it. The best part is they will only follow and listen to my orders."
Ms. Gladstone, in an irritated tone says, "Ok gentlemen, enough of this history lesson. Take a seat and let's wait for the last group to get here."

Shelby, who still has her shield up, smirks and tells everyone that wood shards wouldn't have gotten to them anyway. They all laugh and then they turn the conversation to a more serious topic. They discuss how fast the werewolves are and how pissed Braden is, sitting on the other side of the table. It's as if he could blow at any minute.

Finally, everyone hears the door open and Mr. Beaumont walks in, followed by Raven and his first in command, Dante, and second Amina, followed by Arnoldo and Leo. As they walk towards the table, Shelby reminds Nomed that they can all hear him thinking out loud, but she had to admit Amina is a cutie. Nomed gets up and walks towards Mr. Beaumont and immediately he is stopped by a sword at his neck.

Leo asks, "What is Nomed approaching us for?"

"To introduce myself to this beautiful lady," Nomed says.

Leo smirks and replies, "She doesn't talk to vermin."

Ms. Gladstone tells Nomed to sit down before she makes him sit down, so that they can start with the meeting. Mr. Beaumont stands up and says, "I called this meeting because Raven asked me to and I agreed with his reasoning behind it."

Raven stands as well and says, "Due to the public execution of prized vampires that were given to your houses as a request of good faith, we shouldn't have to sit and see some of our most extraordinary vampires destroyed before we even have a chance to defend them. Our nature is not the same as humans. You guys believe it's a switch we can turn on and off to stop our urges – it is not, and most of all instead of letting me, Bones, or Norie take care of them, you let some newborn of a vampire, someone who we don't know much about his background or origin, handle business that should be taken care of in house."

Ms. Gladstone stands up and says, "Those vampires are our property. We are free to do as we please with them. You have no say so when it comes to this matter…"

"Even though I've played my part in this I have to agree with Raven," Dr. Montague interrupts, "We should let this be handled in house."

Meanwhile inside the shield, everyone is talking and Nomed specifically is the most upset.

"So this is why they called the meeting? Like we weren't requested by these other houses to kill our friends!? I wonder what they would say if they knew neither one of them are dead! I'm sure they wouldn't be agreeing to deal with this in house."

They hear a voice that says, "So Turan and Demetri are alive?" The group freezes in fear as they look around trying to find out who is talking to them. The voice says, "This is Braden. You have nothing to fear and Nomed, maybe you are a nobler vampire than I've given you credit for. I thought you were just a merciless thug."

"How the hell can you talk to us anyway?" Shelby asks.

Braden replies, "I'm the strongest telepath in the world, I can get past your little shield. I've actually been listening to your conversation this entire time, deciding when to kill you because I thought you killed Turan, but I'm sure no one else can get through your shield."

41

Braden goes on, "How about I link you guys into the other chat I'm having with the rest of the prized fighters, because your shield may not be as secure as you think. Amina is a telepath as well, but no one can break into my mental link."

Braden links in Nomed first and he tells everyone how he did not kill Demetri and Turan and it must be kept secret or they will be dooming Nomed and the others. Nomed goes on to tell everyone that they are his family and that he would never harm any of them. He doesn't know much about how he was born but he does know bonds are not meant to be broken. Braden yells, "Nomed say something they are talking to you!"

Nomed looks at Raven and says could you repeat that and Raven says, "Do you agree to not kill anymore vampire without going through me?" Nomed nods in agreement. Raven nods back in affirmation.

Then he states, "Also, I want to have a quick conversation with you before you leave here – just us guys." Once again Nomed nods and Braden links him back to the chat.

"What the fuck? He knows something guys, he has to! Why would he ask to speak to me?" Nomed asked.

Nomed asked Braden to read his mind and Braden replies, "I cannot. He would feel me searching his thoughts. He was one of the original vampires, so he is not acceptable to such things, but I'm sure he doesn't know because only we know your secret."

As the meeting comes to a close, everyone is beginning to gather their things and prepare to leave. Ms. Gladstone, who is upset about the meeting's outcome, storms out the meeting and tells Nomed she will only wait five minutes for them.

As everyone else walks out, Raven comes up to him and ask, "So Nomed, who is your maker and when were you born?"

"I don't remember. I don't know who my maker is either. The only thing I know is that I have this insatiable urge to fight the strongest vampires I come across," Nomed said.

"You can call me Deathscream. Now that everyone is gone, we don't have to be so formal. Honestly, I really hate the formalities. I am more inclined to hearing my name spoken by people and seeing them tremble in fear."

Raven said chuckling as he threw his arm around Nomed's shoulder, "But the real reason I wanted to speak with you was about joining my house and becoming one of my commanders. I will speak to Ms. Gladstone to see if she is willing to confirm you moving if you are curious about learning from the current vampire king on how this whole vampire life, respect, and history goes. Keep in mind Nomed, I won't leave this offer on the table for long."

Raven stood looking at Nomed with an air of confidence under him, knowing without a doubt that Nomed would quickly accept his invitation.

To his surprise, Nomed quickly replied in the opposite, "You don't have to wait long, my answer is no. I would never leave Shelby and Gillie to fend for themselves and survive on their own. If anything was to happen to them I would not be able to live with myself. The offer is tempting, but I am going to have to decline."

As Deathscream laughs he states, "And here I thought you had no morals or loyalty to anyone but Ms. Gladstone. You really are full of surprises Nomed, but still I will give you time to sleep on it and I will send someone to get your answer. Until then, you take care of yourself and hurry back to your plane before everyone leaves you."

Nomed walks out of the tree and looks back at Raven as he shakes his head, laughs and heads off in the opposite direction. As he steps on board of the plane, Ms. Gladstone rushes him and asks him a million questions.

"What was the conversation about between you and Raven? What took you so long? I wonder what is up his sleeve," she said. Nomed could tell she wasn't pleased with what she might have thought was going on.

"Raven just wanted to know who was my maker and invited me to vampire rules school with him," Nomed replied. He proceeds to laugh about the comment he just made, knowing how outlandish it may have sounded. Gladstone turned her nose up at Nomed and walked away.

Just as Ms. Gladstone walked away, Norie walks up and says, "That's not what you guys talked about it, was it?" Nomed tried to play it off, but Norie continued, "I've known him for thousands of millenniums; he asked you to join his house didn't he? Deathscream is always searching for the mightiest of vampires to be under him. So what did you say Nomed?"

Nomed looked her over and said, "For someone who wants nothing to do with me, you sure are mighty talkative right now." "You forget your place?" Norie asks as she interrupts Nomed mid-sentence, "I have no idea what my place is, so I guess you're right. The answer to your question is no. I said no because I would never leave my family to go on missions where they could be killed. It's not like I could rely on anyone else to save them, especially not you," Nomed says.

Out of the gourd on Norie's back, blood starts to come out and in an instant a blade of blood is at Nomed's neck as Norie whispers, "You don't want to get onto my bad side." As Nomed starts to look down Norie's blade, it starts to shake. Norie looks at Nomed in confusion and immediately puts his blood back into his gourd. "We will settle this at a more appropriate time" Norie says.

Nomed turns around and looks at his hand and wonders to himself, *what was that feeling? It seems so familiar to me.* As he walks to sit by Shelby and Gillie, they ask him about what just happened and he says, "I can't really explain it, but I feel as if I've seen it happen before. It's like a technique that's apart of who I am. It's really weird."

 Nomed went on to say, "Also, Raven asked me to become a part of his house, but I declined."

As they land at the house and start departing the plane, Gillie walks up to Nomed and thanks him for not leaving them. Gillie tells Nomed that not too many people would have declined that offer. Nomed smiles and walks onto the roof and just sits thinking about what happened today. As he thinks to himself on how humans look at him as nothing more than a tool to be used as they feel, he says to himself, 'Deathscream might have a valid point of switching sides, but in turn Deathscream has become a puppet himself. He is blindly following the noble houses instead of following his instincts. We were not meant to follow, we were born to lead. Even I know that and I'm a newborn, but one way or another I will free my brothers from this slavery."

Nomed then goes inside and sits in a chair until he falls asleep. When he wakes up, there is a feast in front of him with a card from Ms. Gladstone, thanking him for being loyal to the Horens family for all of these years. Gillie is already eating and Nomed shoots him a dirty look.

"Hey I figured you needed help," Gillie said laughing while chewing the delicious food.

Shelby yells over him, "I told Gillie we should wait but you've been sleep for a long time. Ms. Gladstone wants to see you right after you eat."

"I wonder what she wants now. She is being unusually nice to me since the meeting between all of the houses. Let me scarf down this food and go see what the hell she wants," Nomed says.

Once he is done with his food, he begins to walk down the hall to her office. As he walks in he noticed there is someone already sitting down. Ms. Gladstone welcomes him to sit down and as he does, he notices it is Amina sitting there. She politely says hello to Nomed.

Meanwhile, Ms. Gladstone tells him that Raven sent Amina to talk to him in order to try to get him to join their house, she repeats try.

"So Nomed, she will be following you for the next few weeks just to talk to you and get to know you personally to give the okay for Raven to entertain me with letting you go."

CHAPTER 4
"Pure Bliss"

As Nomed sits with this dumbfounded look on his face, Amina says, "It's funny, I can't read your mind at all. All I feel is this insurmountable power trying to come forth. It's weird, it feels like you have a whole different person inside of you."

"Maybe it's just my inner self thinking about you," Nomed replies. As Amina smirks, she quickly says, "I doubt it."

Nomed gets up and says, "So are you coming with me or do you want to stay with Ms. Gladstone?"

Amina gets up and follows him. In her head she is asking a million questions. She asks where are they going and Nomed says, "To the roof to talk. It's my favorite place to go."

As they walk to the roof, it looks as if there's an entire house on top of the roof. She looks around and sees multiple places to sit or lay down, even a stove and fridge. Amina asks, "Why is it so comfortable on the roof?"

Nomed replies, "Because the view of the stars calms me and I love to come up here and think about life. My question to you Amina is why did Deathscream send you here?"

"Since he didn't tell me not to tell you, I'm really here to find out more about you and what kind of vampire you are. Plus we both know you like me so we are hopeful that fact helps sway you to come to our house," says Amina.

Nomed looks at her with a surprised look on his face and says, "Well if that is the case, ask all the questions you need to."

Amina gets comfortable and begins her list of questions for Nomed.

"Who is your maker? You have to know. We can all feel our maker and know when they are in trouble."

"I've never felt anyone else or a bond. All I know is I woke up hurt in a healing machine from a battle against a vampire where I almost died," Nomed replied.

"Hmm," Amina commented. She then asked, "How did you start working for the Horens?"

"I have been working for the Horens for as long as I can remember. I don't exactly know how we first met or who picked me to work for them. I guess even our kind can lose memories if we are hurt bad enough."

"Have you ever drank the blood of a human?"

"No, they usually give me nectar. They tell me it is the reason why I don't have the urges to kill humans like other vampires."

"Do you truly believe that? It is said that vampires are at their strongest when they do feed on human blood."

"Of course I don't believe that. I just do as they say in order to survive. I truly hate the way humans use us to do their bidding. I have thought over and over about going to a vampire house but they would only pick someone new to fill my spot and no other person can look over Gillie and Shelby like I do. They are the only family I have."

Amina says, "Even Deathscream said you were a noble vampire, and from what you said it seems like you are, so how can you kill prized vampires that you have worked with for ages?"

Nomed replies, "I haven't killed any vampire that didn't deserve it. Next question."

Amina then asked if he had ever been in love. Nomed begins to laugh, "I'm portrayed as a traitor to all vampires, you really think a female vampire on the outside is going to talk to me? That's never going to happen. I've never been on a date before, all I know is missions and the Horens house. I rarely even see Norie when she visits and no one from there even says hello to me."

Amina says, "We will definitely change that since I'm stuck with you for a while."

"I thought you didn't like me," Nomed says.

"I actually thought you were a low down, scumbag, vampire-killing spawn with no sense of self and even though you were cute I didn't think you deserved me even speaking to you; but like I said, I have a habit of reading people's mind by mistake. Perhaps I may have misjudged you."

Amina leans in really close to Nomed and whispers, "Gillie has been watching us out the window, wondering if you are going to tell me about Turan and Demetri for about an hour now. The simple fact that you wouldn't kill your friends and go through so much to hide that they are still alive, while bearing the hate, disgust, and bleak remarks has shown me you are truly a noble and virtuous vampire.

Also, don't worry, your secret is safe with me. I hold no allegiance to anyone. I love my race and would rather see those two alive anyway. My maker was such a loving vampire, which was probably the reason for his death. He cared about vampires too much for his own good. The damned fool tried to lead a revolt against the noble families to free us from their rule but he was found out and they ordered Deathscream to kill him. In turn, they moved me from Norie's vampire house to Deathscream's because he requested to have me moved close to him so that the revolt would be washed away since it would be no one to lead them. Bones' house cleaned out the rest of the commanders with those hellish werewolves that bend to his whim. It was truly one of the darkest nights of my life and it just fills this dark part of my soul. It feels good to know that it's actually another vampire out here that actually cares about his friends and calls them family. Why are you looking that way Nomed?"
He replies, "I'm just in utter awe that you have this side to you. I would have never guessed that you cared so much about vampires and tried to lead a coup against the nobles. It seems like a pretty wicked story. You have to tell me more about it one of these days."

At this point, Gillie can take no more of the conversation between Nomed and Amina. He walks to the roof and tells Nomed, "Don't you think you have been with her long enough? It's only a matter of time before she smooth talks all of the information she needs out of you."

Nomed tells Gillie, "It's nothing more than what you have already told her since you've been watching us. She already heard your thoughts and knows about our not so little secret now."
"I KNEW SOMEONE WAS IN MY HEAD! I could feel it somehow. It felt just like how Braden's powers felt when he linked all our minds." Gillie then looks at Amina and says, "Who gave you permission to go running through my head?" She replies, "Who gave you permission to watch us for as long as you have?"
"I'm not against hitting you."
"You should be. I could sit here and melt your brain for the fun of it."

Nomed steps in and tells them both to play nice. He also reminds Gillie to shield his thoughts better in order for their secret not to come out, just in case Amina was not on their side. Nomed understands Gillie's concern, and it is quite possible that she could tell everyone what they had done.

Nomed then receives a text from Ms. Gladstone telling him to bring his team into the office. As they gather into the room, Ms. Gladstone slides a file across the desk and tells Nomed that she needs him to eliminate a person named Dr. Kegal.

"He used to work for my house but was fired because his methods were way too unorthodox and cruel. He is currently located three hours outside of North Carolina. He is not a vampire, but he has been putting vampire blood into his body and in turn has become a ghoulish human who preys on humans for blood."

"Can Amina come along on this mission?"

Ms. Gladstone says, "Of course. You're babysitting her anyway, not me."

Amina rolls her eyes at Ms. Gladstone and says, "I'll fly the plane. Let's go guys." During the flight, Shelby sits right next to Amina on the plane and says, "You know he's like my brother, right? I will kill you if you hurt him."

"Even though my first instinct was to kick him until he breaks, I've actually grown quite fond of him. You could even say I like him a little. Now get ready, we are here."

At first glance, the building looks like a rundown old mill but as Gillie picks the lock to the front door, they open it and see that the building on the inside is totally new. It looks like a space-age science facility – everything looks very high-tech and new, as if this was the first time anyone has ever been there before. Nomed tells Shelby to put a shield around them, because there is no telling what kind of things will happen in this facility.

As they walk around, they see all kinds of monstrosities. Humans barely alive in tubes and cryogenic-baths, along with blood being splashed around everywhere. It reeks of pain and despair and all in the air you can tell whatever is going on here has definitely been unpleasant for all of the test subjects. Just then, the front door closes and a voice comes over the intercom.

"So that coward Gladstone sent you guys to take care of me, huh? Don't worry, I have plenty of surprises in store for you guys. I would like you guys to meet vampits – they are pit bulls with the genes of vampires spliced into them, which has given them extraordinary powers."

Down the hall, they see three hellish pit bulls running towards them. One is made out of stone, one is made out of a type of crystal, and the other is breathing fire. Nomed tells Shelby to step back and put the shield around her, then he tells Amina to step behind him. She laughs and says, "I can take care of myself," as she pulls two hand held knives from behind her back. She cockily asks Nomed, "Which one do you prefer?" Nomed looks and says, "I'll take the one breathing fire."

Gillie rushes towards the dog made out of crystal. As it leaps towards him, he disappears and shows up behind the dog, gliding in the air and pulls his gun. The next thing you see is a shiny black bullet piercing the dog's skull. As Gillie touches the ground he says, "The other two are yours." Anima rushes the one made of stone and as it leaps, she gracefully flips over it while kicking it to the ground.

At the same time, Nomed puts his hands in his pockets and slowly walks toward the dog that has fire drooling from its mouth. It starts growling at Nomed, causing fire to blow in Nomed's face. Nomed starts to laugh and says, "I've seen worse beasts than you!" He grabs the pit by the mouth with both hands while taking all of the flames to his face. With his brute strength, he rips the dog in half while throwing both pieces behind him, while he sits on top of a table near him. He looks over at Amina and yells, "Amina, could you be any slower?"

"I was just getting warmed up," she says as she back pedals from the dog trying to chomp at her legs. She then stops and puts both swords together and they become one and she slices the dog into hundreds of little pieces. Then with her sword, she hits the last piece up in the sky and with a twirling kick launches it towards Nomed, who only moves out the way just in time. He looks at her and rolls his eyes, "Nice try."

Shelby then walks up and says, "Now that that's over, I guess we should continue through this creepy shit hole now." Nomed yells out, "Is that all you got, Dr. Kegal?" There is a sinister chuckle as Dr. Kegal says, "Don't be in such a rush to meet your death. I have plenty more experiments waiting for you." Suddenly, all the lights point towards one door.

"Are we really going to walk straight into a trap?" Amina asks.

"This wouldn't be any fun if we didn't at least let him think he had us where he wants us," Nomed replied.

As they step into the room, it has sun rays beaming towards them. Shelby immediately puts a shield around them and Nomed tells Gillie to shoot out all of the lights. Gillie sighs, "I didn't plan on working this hard today" as he grabs his gun and shoots a black bullet towards one of the lights. As it hits the first light it splits off into multiple angles hitting the rest of the lights as well. Nomed says to Gillie, "You know, if you weren't so lazy you could be an elite vampire." Gillie replies, "I'm already an elite vampire! Just because I don't show you all of my abilities doesn't mean I don't know how to practice in my free time."

As he finishes his sentence, a door opens up and Dr. Kegal appears. He says, "It seems I underestimated this group. Enough of the games. I guess it's best that I meet you all directly." As they walk closer, a skinny scientist in a white lab coat is standing in front of them with a sadistic look on his face. He is smiling so much that there is a pool of drool that has formed in the corner of his mouth. In his hand he has a glass tube that has a red and green substance in it. He looks over at Nomed and says, "Nomed, let's leave everyone else out of this. Let us fight – just me and you, one on one." Nomed says confidently, "You don't look like you could handle any of us, to be honest with you."

Dr. Kegal then drinks the vile that he has had in his hand and his body begins to mutate into this monstrosity of a man. Nomed walks up to him and realizes he is now an entire person shorter than him. Nomed is still unphased. He stands up to him, with a smirk on his face, and he says, "Is this all the powering up you can do?" Dr. Kegal punches at Nomed and Nomed swings also in immediate retaliation.

As their fists meet, there is a standstill. Nomed begins to smirk and says, "This should be a fun test." Dr. Kegal then uses all his force to hit Nomed. He is hit so hard in his ribs that his body bends inward and he is blast through the wall.

Amina pulls out her blades and runs towards Dr. Kegal, but she is stopped by an invisible shield. As she looks back, Shelby says, "Don't be worried about him, he has been through worse. Just let him fight. If you interrupt him, he will be mad."
Gillie cuts in and says, "Yeah, last time I butted in he hit me along with the bad guy."

Dr. Kegal looks at Amina and says, "So you're mad that I broke your boyfriend." Behind him, a slab of concrete is thrown at Dr.

Kegal. As it hits him in the head, Nomed says, "Pay attention to the fight in front of you," as he pulls himself out of the rubble from the wall. Nomed yells and speeds towards Dr. Kegal. As they meet it is an onslaught of give and take punches. The brute force behind them are cracking and bending the floor and places around them. Nomed says in between punches, "At this rate we are going to destroy your little laboratory." Dr. Kegal yells through his maniacal laughter, "I will rebuild it all on top of your corpses."

Amina realized someone is headed their way and tells Shelby and Gillie they should be expecting someone and that he is fast. As soon as she finishes her statement, Calderon shows up behind them and says, "Well I see Nomed hasn't changed one bit."
"What are you doing here? You're lucky I didn't shoot you," Gillie says to Calderon.
"I was sent here to destroy the entire building after you guys got rid of Dr. Kegal.
Gillie jumps in and says, "So in other words, you're just here for clean-up?"
"Exactly and to watch a good fight of course."

As they look back at the fight, Nomed and Dr. Kegal have thrown each other out the window. As they fall to the ground everyone else just walks over to the ledge and takes a sit down. Calderon laughs and says, "Well, at least we have sky box tickets to the fight now."

As Nomed charges towards Dr. Kegal, Dr. Kegal yells and Nomed can see the waves coming towards him. He dodges the attack. As he looks back, he can see that the trees behind him are being blown away. As he closes in he can hear Amina in his head, *"This is getting boring. Can you stop playing so we can go do something fun?"* Nomed replies back, "Why didn't you say something earlier?" Without realizing, Nomed stopped moving completely. By the time he notices, Dr. Kegal has punched him deep into the ground and begins to yell sending sonic waves right towards him. Next thing you know, Nomed comes from under the ground behind him and grabs him by the head and throws him into the ground. With his other hand, he crushes Dr. Kegal's larynx as he says, "I guess you won't be able to do all that screaming anymore.

Dr. Kegal attempts to throw punches towards Nomed and his punch is blocked, Nomed breaks his arm. Nomed says, "You might have tried to become one of us but you will never be one of us you filthy human," as he punches out his heart.

Calderon floats down on a gust of wind and says, "I really enjoy seeing you fight. I never really go on group missions with you guys anymore. I miss that." Gillie, Shelby, and Amina all jump out of the building to the ground and walk over telling Nomed he could have finished the fight earlier. Calderon then takes two of the orbs from his belt – one that looks like fire and the other like dirt. He breaks them and lifts the contents in the sky and as he mixes them together, they create a black flame. As he moves it towards the building, moving it back and forth, it immediately incinerates everything it touches. The building is gone in minutes.

Next, Calderon throws the flame onto Dr. Kegal's dead body and in seconds it is completely gone.

After Calderon is finished, he says, "It was nice working with you guys" and he lifts himself on a cloud of air and flies off in the sky. Just as quickly as he came, he was gone.

CALDERON

Amina then says, "Come on guys, let's get ready to go back" as she jumps in the plane and fires up the engine. As they all get back to the Horens house, Amina tells Gillie and Shelby to get out and tells Nomed to stay. When everyone walks out, Nomed asks why they are still sitting on the plane. Amina says, "This is going to be our first date. We are going to see the Eiffel Tower." They both exchange coy smiles. Inside, his heart is racing because he's never been on a date before.

As they travel across the world, and they get closer and closer to the Eiffel Tower, Nomed can feel his inner youth starting to kick in. He is full of excitement and it helps that he is on a trip with someone he likes. She parks on top of a roof and they jump down and begin to walk around. The entire time they are walking, Nomed is amazed by the people out in the streets having fun and living life.
"Have you ever been this free? Just being able to go wherever you want and do whatever you want without being bossed around like a dog?" Before Dracula disappeared, we all had that type of freedom. To be one with the night, to have fun, to walk around freely; those were the good ole days.

As they got in front of the Eiffel Tower, Nomed grabs her in his arms and jumps up to the top of the tower. As they sit and watch the city, they continue to learn about each other. She goes on to tell him how Raven created her father and since his death he has kept a close eye on her. Feeling vulnerable, Nomed even goes on to tell her he has never had anyone to look over him ever in life. The stories continue to go on and on for hours, until Amina says, "We better start heading back to the house before the sun comes out and we both go before our time."

As they get back to the Horens house, Nomed passes out in the first chair he can find. Amina then asks Shelby, "Why does Nomed never sleep in a normal place? Does he always just fall asleep wherever he chooses?"
"Ever since I've known Nomed, I've known him to be this way. He sleeps in places where he won't be alone or that people can easily find him because he says it gives everyone a safe feeling knowing he is somewhere where he can easily be seen." Amina looks over at Nomed as he is now fast asleep and snoring. Everyone has had an exhausting day, so Amina decides to go get some sleep as well.

The next day as Amina wakes up, Nomed is standing in front of her and tells her to get up because they are going to the movies. She looks up and tells Nomed, "It's hours before the sun goes down." "That's what's wrong with all you vampires, you sleep too much when you could be doing something important. Get ready, I'll see you downstairs."

As she walks down stairs she asks, "So how are we going to get to the movies?"
"I helped build back ways to places that I like to visit and my favorite thing to do is watch movies, so follow me, we're going to the movies," Nomed said.

He leads her to a secret hallway that lights up just enough for them to see. As she follows behind him she asks, "So how many places do the hallways lead to?"
Nomed says, "I can get anywhere within a ten mile radius but the main places I go are to the movies, games, and fights."
"So in other words, you enjoy everything dealing with action. So what are we watching anyway?"
"An action movie, of course," Nomed says as he starts to laugh.
As they get there, they come through a back passage and they are directly in the movie theater's seating area.
"Do you need anything? Refreshments? Bathroom? None of those things are by the light, so I can go get them for you," Nomed says.
"No, I'm fine for now, thank you."
They sit for a while and after a few minutes Amina does decide to go to the bathroom and get snacks right before the movie begins. She also gets Nomed a bottle of nectar.
"I didn't know this place was vampire friendly."
"Yeah, I got Ms. Gladstone to work something out with them, so they keep special snacks and nectar for us." Nomed looked down at the bottle of nectar and says, "I've never had anyone buy anything for me before, thank you."
"I'm sure you have never met someone like me before then," Amina says.

The movie seemed to last forever, but they sat there laughing and thoroughly enjoying the movie. When the movie was over and they left Amina said, "Let's go on a vacation. I know that you have never taken one."
"Sure, I'll tell Ms. Gladstone I'll be gone for a few days."

"Tell her more like a couple of months. You need a break from life."
Nomed hesitates, but smiles and says, "Of course. Let's do it."

As they get back to the Horens house he types up a letter and goes to hand it to Ms. Gladstone. After he hands it over he says, "If you need me just call, but I will be gone for a while."
Ms. Gladstone looked at him with an upset look on her face, "It's no stopping you this time, is it Nomed?"
"No, I really need to do this; but I'll be back."

He goes and tells Gillie and Shelby that he will be leaving and not to go on any missions without him. They all engage in a big hug, and then Nomed is on his way.

Amina and Nomed then leave. They go to a small island that is only populated by vampires.
"What kind of place is this?" Nomed asks Amina.
"This is a vampire retreat. My father created it before he passed away. It is a judgment-free zone for all vampires. We are not allowed to talk about anything going on in the outside world here. Plus, it is always as dark as the night sky here. Come on, follow me."

They walk up to a beachfront house that they will be staying in for the next couple weeks. Their time on the island was spent just talking and laughing as they dug deeper into each other's secrets and entire lives. Nomed opens up to her completely and tells her things he has never told anyone. One day, they go into the island's market and Nomed buys her this small gold chain with a golden cross. Amina says, "This is beautiful even though it is so controversial to our entire being I love it."

As they walk into the house Amina stops and looks into Nomed's eyes. Immediately, they begin to kiss, and as they do, they float around the house touching and kissing. The feelings they have for each other seems like they can last forever at this point.

As they lay on the roof Nomed tells Amina, "I could do this with you for the rest of my life." He tells her he doesn't want to work at the Horens house anymore, he wants to just live free and roam the world with her.
Amina replies, "As noble as that is, Raven nor Ms. Gladstone will never let that happen."
Nomed replies back to her, "Then we will make them."

11 months later….

"Gillie! Shelby! Come here now," Ms. Gladstone yells. Gillie and Shelby come to Ms. Gladstone, ready to meet her demand.

"I need you to go out and check on Nomed. It's been almost twelve months and he has not returned. I activated the tracker on his phone so that I could locate him. Here are his coordinates. Can you just make sure he is ok? Give him this card for me."

Gillie and Shelby do not argue or complain. They take the card and coordinates and prepare to find their brother, as they have missed him terribly as well.

As they board the plane Shelby says to Gillie, "Is it just me, or is it weird that Ms. Gladstone has been so nice lately? Is it bothering you like it is me?"

"It does feel like something is up her sleeve," Gillie says.

As they go to the end to jump out the plane Gillie says, "Where is the island?" Shelby says, "It's inside the mountain. How else do you think it stays night all the time there?" As they walk into the retreat, they ask the people where to find Nomed and they point them in the right direction.

As they approach the house, Nomed and Amina meet them at the front door. Nomed is all smiles as he sees his closest family has come to see him. They all go in and sit down. Gillie and Shelby tell Nomed they have missed him and that the Horens house is different without him being there. Shelby hands Nomed the card Ms. Gladstone gave her, "Ms. Gladstone wanted me to give you this."

He opens it and tells them what it says, "She says that she has missed us, but also that she is requesting that I return."

"Well, is that something you want to do? I mean, come on man, it's been twelve months already, don't you think you have vacationed enough?" Gillie says.

"Well, since we are on that subject, I think we should all leave the Horens house and just live our own lives; what do you guys think?"

"First off, Ms. Gladstone will never let that happen, but we are with you no matter what you decide. We always will be on your side so your decision is our decision," Shelby said.

"Yeah, at the end of the day, we are family, so if you want us to leave Ms. Gladstone, then we should leave. I never liked her anyways," Gillie chimed in. The three of them looked at one another and smiled. Gillie and Shelby could tell that Nomed was happy here with

Amina. In some odd way, they longed for their own freedom as well, and maybe this was their chance at that freedom.

At the Horens house, Ms. Gladstone slams her fist down on the desk saying, "I knew putting that recording device on that cards' stamp was a good thing."

She had just overheard the agreement for Nomed, Gillie and Shelby to potentially leave her house. In a rage, she calls Raven on the phone. When Raven answers, Ms. Gladstone wastes no time plotting her revenge on Nomed. "We have to get rid of Amina," she says.

"Why?!" Raven yells.

"Because ever since she came around, she has caused nothing but problems! She has Nomed wanting to leave the Horens house now and he plans to take Gillie and Shelby with him!"

Raven is apprehensive about the idea immediately, "Are you sure this is the only way to solve this? I have already killed her father, I cannot kill her as well. Why don't you get Bones to have the werewolves take care of her?"

Ms. Gladstone hangs up the phone on Raven and screams. She cannot believe he is not on board with this plan. Meanwhile, Raven sits and proceeds to pour up a drink, knowing he just condemned his commander to death.

As Nomed and the rest of the team makes it back to the Horens house, Ms. Gladstone meets them and with the most convincing demeanor, she says, "Nomed and Amina, it is good to see you guys! Amina, I wish you all could stay for a while, but Raven wants you back at the Talos vampire house. He says he has an important covert mission for you."

Amina kisses Nomed and tells him that she will be back as soon as she can and tells him she loves him. Nomed stands in front of her, astonished at her expression of love to him, "I love you too, Amina."

They exchange smiles and as Amina gets on the plane, she looks over at Nomed one last time, promising him that she will return.

CHAPTER 5
"The Order"

As Nomed walks back into the building, he jokingly asks Ms. Gladstone if he was missed. "You didn't even call me while I was gone," Nomed laughs.

"You're lucky I didn't come to get you a long time ago. You haven't even been on a mission for a year, but that is ok because I have one for you. Your next mission for me will be to protect my son, Jonathan. He has a night game he needs to get to and return home from."

Nomed rolls his eyes and scoffs, "Are you serious? Couldn't Gillie or Shelby have done this while I was gone?"

"First, don't question me. Second, didn't you tell them not to go on any missions while you were gone? They follow your instructions without flaw or question."

"Fine, fine. I'm sorry. I'll do it." Ms. Gladstone goes to get Jonathan to make sure he is ready for his game. After a few minutes of waiting, Jonathan and Nomed are ready and they finally depart.

While Nomed is being Ms. Gladstone's personal babysitter, he starts to text Amina.

"So, what important mission did Raven have for you when you got to Talos?"

She replies back, "He has me here in Russia trying to find a vampire killer that is on the run. It could take months to find him in his home country!" Nomed could feel the tone of her text was frustration. He felt the same.

"Need any help? My mission is far less complicated than yours. I could use a challenge." She replies, "Raven already said you couldn't come help because you're too loud when it comes to fighting and it would be all over the news in no time. He says we don't need that type of attention."

"You know what? You have a point there, I usually don't hold back in fights." Amina tells Nomed that she has to get back to her mission, but will call him when she can. Nomed smiles, puts his phone away and gets back to watching Jonathan play his game.

About another thirty minutes goes by before Nomed and Jonathan are finally on their way back to the Horens house. On the way home, Nomed asks the driver to make a quick stop at the shopping center. He jumped out and told Jonathan that he would be right back. As he gets back in the car Jonathan asks, "Who did you buy something for?"

Nomed replies, "It's for my lady friend."

They pull back up to the house and he says, "Alright, let's get you back to your mom before she tries to kill me." As he walks in he asks where Gillie and Shelby are. The guards tell him they are on the roof. As he walks onto the roof he is smiling from ear to ear.

"I guess you just got off the phone with Amina, huh lover boy?" Gillie says.

"For your information, I did talk to her today, but that is not the reason I'm smiling. Check this out!" He pulls out a box and opens it. As Gillie and Shelby walk closer they realize it's an all red ring that is so perfectly shaped they have nothing to say.

Shelby finally speaks and says, "When do you plan on asking her to marry you?"

He replies, "Whenever she comes to visit again."

They make one of the guards go get a bottle of champagne as they begin to spend their night celebrating and laughing about the good times. The next day, Nomed goes to see Ms. Gladstone. He walks straight into her office and tells her that they will be leaving. "Shelby, Gillie and I will be leaving. You will have to find a new team of prized fighters."

Ms. Gladstone yells, "You have the audacity to come in barking at me about what you're going to do like you're in charge!"

Nomed does not budge as she walks up to him and stands next to him. She says the incantation *"alon tatarus demon"*, and in no time Nomed is on the ground in pain. He begins to say through tears of agony, "No matter how much pain you put me through I won't work for you. No matter what happens to me, you know my team is loyal to a fault, and they will honor our agreement to not work for you either."

Ms. Gladstone looks at him with an evil glare, as if she wants to kill Nomed right in the spot she put him down.

"Don't forget Ms. Gladstone, if anything happens to me, Gillie can shift time and we can set the time back prior to you even uttering the incantation."

With that being said, she releases him and says, "You're so weak. All it took was a woman and a year and you are tired of working for me. That is fine, I am sure there are better prized fighters than you three anyway. When are you leaving?"

As Nomed picks himself up off of the ground he says, "As soon as Amina returns, me and my team are leaving and he walks out."

It's been four months since Amina has left and Nomed has been able to talk to her on the phone. Nomed is beginning to worry about her and wonders if he should try and find her. Whenever he calls, she doesn't answer or doesn't have time to talk. As he calls her, hoping for a different response on this day than previous days, she picks up and says, "Hey I'm close to finding the hunter, I will have to call you as soon as I finish this task."

"Wait! Can you at least tell me you're doing ok?"

"I'm doing ok, Nomed. I promise I will be home soon. This task may mean I can actually come home to you," Amina says.

Nomed hangs up the phone on his end, hoping that what she says is true. Meanwhile, Amina hears screams from an ally way. As she jumps down from the roof top, she sees two red flashes and in front of her are the werewolves' king and queen. The king steps up to Amina and says, "Well hello. My name is Tunstall and this is Tala. I see you finally caught up with us. We have been making you run in circles for months to make it seem like an accident, so when Nomed finds out that you're dead, it will look like a murder."

Amina looks at them confused, "What in the hell are you talking about? The only ones dying today are you."

"That is our order as you know we can't disobey an order. Bones has a pretty strict rule on this. We have to follow orders as if they were absolute and it sucks that we know you have found love with Nomed and all. In our world, that is hard to come by. I'm sorry we have to kill you."

Tala then speaks, "We will give you one request, as long as it is not to live."

Amina says, "So the Horens house put you guys up to this because they were scared Nomed would leave, huh? Is this Ms. Gladstone's sad excuse for getting me out of the way?"

"That is the sad truth. They wanted you out of the way and Raven could not bring himself to do it since he killed your father so they sent us, but once again, what is your request?" Tunstall says.

"If this will be my fate, my only request is that you let me record a message to Nomed before you kill me."

Tala walks up and says, "We will accept your request and we will make sure to make it quick."

Amina, with tears in her eyes, starts to record a message for Nomed.

"Nomed, I just want you to know I love you and that this past year has been nothing short of amazing with you. The hunters I ran into are way stronger than myself and out of mercy they allowed me to send this message. All I can say is don't trust anyone but your friends and don't mourn for me. Let this be a happy time for you and most of all, lead your family, the prized vampires, to a better life. Just know Nomed, I died with no pain and that knowing I found the vampire of my dreams. When I thought it was never possible you put my soul to rest. Once again Nomed, I love you. Goodbye my love." Amina hits send on the message.

Tala moves behind her and Tunstall to the front and they decapitate her with a double lariat.

Meanwhile Nomed, Gillie, and Shelby are sitting at the table as a message comes in on Nomed's phone. He picks up his phone and realizes it's a voice message from Amina. Nomed and the team freeze as they listen to the message. As soon as he hears the beginning part, Nomed drops his phone and like a flash of light, he runs out the building and rushes over to the Talons vampire house. He makes it there faster than the speed of light. In a fit of rage, he breaks open the gigantic door in front of the house, and Raven is at the door to meet him.

"Not only are you loud, but you are disrespectful as well. What the fuck brings you here?" Raven says. Nomed breathing heavily says, "I need the tracker to Amina's location and if you deny me, I will kill everyone here."

"As much as I would like to see you try, I have no problem handing that over." He walks Nomed into the house and leads him to where he has his setup for Amina's tracker. "Here is my assistant. Please look up Amina's location for him."

Nomed sees the location and rushes off to where she is. As he gets to her location, all he sees is her body lying there. Nomed drops down on his knees and lets out a yell that shakes the buildings around them. As the tears flow down his face, he looks down at the ground

and he sees the chain he bought Amina and immediately he is filled with rage. Nomed begins knocking down buildings and anything that gets in his way. As he works on continuing to level the block, Raven appears in front of him and he tells Nomed to calm down.
"MOVE OUT OF THE WAY OR I WILL KILL YOU!" Nomed screams as he knocks Raven through a building.

Next thing you know, Raven blindsides him and knocks him in the middle of the street, "Let's do this the easy way. I don't want to hurt you, Nomed."
"I don't care. Kill me if you have to!" Nomed replies as he charges towards him.

Raven lifts his hands as if he was shooting a gun and instantly, both of his arms fly off his body. By the time he reaches Raven, he is completely bloody. As he leans in he just places his head on Raven's shoulder and passes out. Raven takes his body back to Ms. Gladstone. When Gillie and Shelby see Nomed they go into a rage and charge Raven.

Ms. Gladstone says the incantation and instantly both of them are on the ground in pain and Ms. Gladstone tells them, "I know you guys are upset, but let's be real here. If Nomed could not defeat him do you really think the two of you can? Plus Nomed will heal and be okay in no time; so I'm about to release you guys and I would advise you not to try that again. Matter of fact, make yourselves useful and take Nomed to his room so that he can heal."
Gillie looks at Raven and says, "Why weren't you caught in the incantation like us?" Raven replies, "Mind your business and go take him to his room."

Four months pass by and Shelby finally calls Braden over to the Horens house to ask him why Nomed isn't healing like he should. Braden looks at her and Gillie and says, "A vampire has to want to heal in order for the process to start. Nomed has lost his will to live and doesn't want to heal. These wounds and body parts should have grown back overnight."
Gillie says, "We know you can do it. What is he thinking about over there?" Braden looks at Nomed and begins to read his mind. He tells them, "He is thinking of Amina and reliving that day over and over, but I will go into his thoughts and tell him that he still has family waiting on him and worried about his well-being."

Braden goes into his thoughts and relays the message. Braden says, "Let's leave and give him some time to ponder on what I said to him." As they all walk out, Nomed finally opens his eyes and just stares at the wall. He begins to cry tears of blood, as the only thing he is playing back in his head is the scene where he finds Amina's body lying lifeless on the ground.

The next day Gillie walks in and sees that Nomed is awake. He says, "I've been waiting for you to wake up. I would hand this to you but you would have to grow your arms back for that, so I'll just put it on for you. This is the chain Amina had on when she was killed. I kind of shifted time at her funeral as I was walking by, so I could grab it for you, I hope you don't mind."

After five months of not speaking, Nomed finally speaks and says, "Thank you Gillie. You are the best brother I could ask for." Gillie nods his head and gets up and walks out. The next morning, as Shelby and Gillie are sitting at the table, Nomed walks in and sits down. Shelby smiles and says, "It's good to have you back. I see you put her ring on her chain it looks very nice, Nomed. She would have loved it."

Nomed says, "I couldn't agree more. I just wanted to show you guys that I'm better. I'll see ya later." As he gets up and walks out, he walks through the house and runs into Ms. Gladstone. She grabs him by his head and gives him a hug while saying, "I'm so deeply sorry for your loss."

Nomed says thank you and he heads to the bar. He tells one of the servants to hand him the two strongest bottles of alcohol with a cup of ice.

With both bottles in hand, Nomed goes to the roof. As Gillie and Shelby meet him up there, they realize Nomed is completely drunk and has been mixing the two bottles of alcohol together. Shelby walks up and tries to take the bottle. Nomed looks at her with a look so terrifying she immediately retracts her hand. They decide to leave the roof and allow Nomed to wallow in his pity.

The next couple of weeks Nomed begins to sit in random corners or on the floor around the house and drink all day. He hasn't changed clothes or asked to leave the house. It is as if Nomed has fallen into a black hole and has no intention of coming back. He always has a blank stare on his face and never really seems to be paying attention to anything that's going on around him, unless someone has taken his bottle of liquor. After days of watching him, Gillie and Shelby go sit down beside him on the floor and they both have cups. Nomed says "Why did you guys bring me a cup. I don't need it."

Gillie replies, "The cups aren't for you, they are for us. If you're going to drink your life away we are going to do the same."

Shelby chimes in and says, "Yeah, so I guess I need to tell Braden I won't see him for a while. I have to bury myself in a few bottles. Also, just to let you know all of the prized vampires said they are with you if you want to go find Amina's killer."

Shelby tosses Nomed his phone, "Here is your phone. I think you should actually listen to the last message Amina sent you. She wouldn't want you to sit around like this. She wants you to be a leader and to make more of yourself than just a slave running errands. How can you lead us when you are a miserable drunk that doesn't care about his future? Now pour my damn drink, you pansy."

"Wow! I think she's been waiting to tell you all that," Gillie says while laughing.

Nomed gives Shelby a slight smirk and pours her a cup of liquor as they all sit back and enjoy a good laugh.

CHAPTER 6
"The Decision"

As dusk turns to dawn, Ms. Gladstone comes up to Nomed, "Hey, I know you quit, but could you watch my son for a few weeks? He really looks up to you."

"I have no reason to leave here anymore; I will be here long after you are gone so it might be a good thing that he likes me."

Ms. Gladstone then says, "He will be here tomorrow, Nomed. Oh, and one more thing, no more drinking! You have had enough of that going on to last an eternity and I don't want you doing that shit around my son."

"Fine, after we finish this bottle I won't touch another one. I finally remembered I have to live the life Amina wanted me to."

The next day Ms. Gladstone's son Jonathan walks up to Nomed at Horens house. Nomed couldn't tell if he was excited to be with him or not. Jonathan looks at Nomed and says, "I guess you are my bodyguard from now on Big bro. I have nothing to do during the summertime so I'll sleep when you sleep and we can go out during the night since I don't have to worry about anything happening to me." Nomed laughs and just says to him, "So what? You want to be a vampire, huh?"

Ms. Gladstone overhears Nomed talking to Jonathan and interrupts them, "Don't even put those type of crazy things into his head. He has to be able to lead this house when I am gone! No one else is fit to sit at the throne of such a pivotal house." Nomed rolls his eyes at Ms. Gladstone, looks down and says, "Come on kid, let's go shoot some hoops in the gym."

As they reach the workout section of the house, Nomed tells Jonathan to go inside and start shooting while he stays back for a moment. He pulls out his phone and replays Amina's last video to him. The portion about not trusting anyone but your friends sticks out in his head the most each time he replays it. Nomed puts the phone back in his pocket and goes inside to start playing with Jonathan.

As they are shooting around at the gym, Nomed is interrogating Jonathan without him even realizing it – asking questions about the house and if he knows of any good places to go and hide if he needs to. Jonathan; who is oblivious to the line of questioning, goes on to say, "Of course, but my mom made me promise not to tell anyone where that place was so I can't tell you, Mr. Nomed."

"Oh, ok" Nomed says. He brushes it off, but in his head, Nomed is devising a way to make the boy tell him where this location is and he came to the conclusion to become this boy's best friend. Every day and every night, Nomed plays and entertains Jonathan with whatever he wants to do. Also when Ms. Gladstone gets mad or doesn't let him do things, Nomed goes behind her back and lets him do the things he wants to do, which begins to make Jonathan open up to him more and more.

As weeks go by, they pretty much become attached to each other by the hip. One day, Gillie and Shelby call Nomed into a room and ask him, "Why are you spending so much time with her son? Is this some type of coping syndrome or do you actually like this little boy?"

"When we first started hanging out, he mentioned a room here that only the humans know about that his mom said he could go hide if he ever needed to or if anything happened to her and it has the records of everything he would need to know and that is what I'm interested in learning from him, so if I have to play day care that's what I will do in order to get some answers about what they have been hiding from us. Until then, we are all going to play nice and act like we are all having the best time of our lives."

As soon as he finishes that statement, Jonathan walks in the door and ask can they go to the basketball game tonight. Nomed says sure and they both walk out the door.

For the next four months, Nomed spends his time going to every game, party, and trip Jonathan asks him to go. Since he was with Ms. Gladstone's son, she didn't take on any missions for Nomed. They went to the other noble houses, which in turn gave Nomed more time to strictly focus on manipulating this boy to show him to this secret place.

In time, Jonathan finally opens up to Nomed and tells him the place is located on the property under the fountain in the middle of the garden. Also, he lets Nomed know that no one can get in at night other than Ms. Gladstone. The fountain is only opened during the day for noble visitors and people of that nature. After finding this out, he immediately goes to Shelby and asks her to take him there so he can look into it. She says yes and laughs.

"Next time, don't take almost a year to find out some information. We could have gotten Braden to find that info out in no time." Nomed replies, "Ms. Gladstone has had work done on all the nobles' heads so that no one can read their minds. I must say it is a great feat and sadly smart as fuck, so with him telling me that, I'm sure Braden could have read his mind, but Jonathan would have known that Braden was reading his thoughts. Then his mom would have probably tried to hang all of us."

Nomed tells her Jonathan has a soccer game tomorrow during the day and everyone will be away so they can try to sneak into the room then. The next morning, Nomed is waiting for Shelby at the door as the group of cars head to the game. As they walk out the door, Shelby reminds Nomed that her shield can only cover them for fifteen minutes. They have to make it quick or else they will both die. As they run through the acres of land before the house they finally reach the fountain at the front of the property. Nomed is frantically trying to find a switch or lever that opens up the secret passage.

Finally, he finds the key and he notices that the angel statue wing on the fountain can be pulled down. When he pulls it, the fountain separates and there are stairs that lead down. Shelby reminds him that once they come back up they only have two minutes to make it back to the house before her shield will disappear. As they walk down the stairs, they get to a door. Nomed tries to pry it open but it's not coming open. Then he sees the fingerprint scanner by the door. "Fuck!" he yells, "I'm sure only someone from the noble blood line can get in here. Let's get out of here as fast as we can."

Shelby and Nomed dart out of the room and run as fast as they can back across the acres of land. As they almost reach the door, Shelby's shield runs out. She looks back at Nomed. He senses the fear in her eyes and he hurdles her through the door and instantly throws his jacket over his head. As his fingers begin to burn and catch on fire while he is holding his jacket, he runs as fast as he can to the door. He burst through the door leaving a trail of smoke behind him as he hits the ground right by Shelby. They look up and Gillie is crouched over standing on a table, eating an apple.

"So, that was a close one," Gillie says.

Shelby replies, "Gillie you are an asshole. We almost died."

Nomed just begin to laugh and says, "You have a point there. Good thing I always wear a jacket or half of my face might be missing right now."

"So what did you find out about the secret room?" Gillie asks.

"The way to get in is with the angel wing on the fountain. The only problem is that the door is protected by a thumb print and can't be opened any other way, so I have no choice but to make Jonathan lead me to the room himself. That will be the only way I will get in for sure, but I don't know how to actually make that happen so I will continue to work on his trust until he finally breaks in and leads me to the building."

"Or you could just fake an attack on the building and make him go there for hiding. That would be brilliant!" Gillie begins to laugh. As he stops laughing, he looks down at Nomed's face. It's as if Gillie had the most amazing idea of his life.

"Oh shit, you can't be serious! You are actually going to take that suggestion seriously?"

"What do we have to lose?"

"Our lives!! How the hell do you plan to have that play out with Ms. Gladstone here? It would never work."

Nomed says, "Let me think on that. When I come up with a plan I will tell you what it is. If you are not comfortable with it we can scratch the idea and go back to the drawing board. Deal?" Nomed stretched out his fist and Gillie fist bumps him to seal the deal.

Three days later, Nomed calls them to the roof and tells Shelby to put up her shield and as she does he tells them that the best way to have Ms. Gladstone leave is to request that they all stop being prized fighters and that they will be moving to a Raven house.

"With all three of us wanting to leave, she will have to meet in order to come up with the decision between all of the noble houses. On top of that, they will have to go all the way to the Talos vampire house to speak with Raven, which should take a day or two. They won't invite us because the topic of discussion is us."

Shelby and Gillie look confused, but let Nomed continue, "I will get Demetri and Turan to act as the intruders in masks so that it looks like I'm actually in grave danger and I will make Jonathan run to the safe place when I tell him."

Shelby interrupts and says, "You know what, Nomed? That's a great idea! I think that may actually work in our favor. So when are you going to tell her?"

Nomed says, "I'm going to tell her tonight so hopefully she leaves tomorrow morning and calls an emergency meeting. I will call Demetri and Turan as I'm sure they will be all for it. I actually decided I was going to do it before you guys said yes."

"So after you get him out of the room how are you going to get him to just let you search around is my question," Gillie says skeptically.

"You know what, I didn't even think of that to tell the truth," Nomed says.

Shelby says, "Why don't I just put a shield around his head until he passes out?"

"Shelby that's cruel, but I will allow it so that we don't have to hurt him in order to shut him up," Gillie says.

Gillie turns to Nomed and says, "So Nomed, when are you going to decide to tell her all of this so we can get the ball rolling?"

Nomed simply replies, "Now."

The Decision

Nomed walks out of the room and walks directly into Ms. Gladstone's office. She looks at him and adamantly demands, "What do you want Nomed? I have a long night ahead of me."

Nomed takes a deep breath and thinks, *"here goes nothing."*

"Shelby, Gillie, and I are requesting to be moved to the Talos vampire house under Raven's care and be replaced with new prized vampires."

Ms. Gladstone looks up at Nomed and says, "You're such an ungrateful little shit! You have some nerve coming in here and telling me you're leaving."

Nomed interrupts and says, "This is our right to ask to leave and be replaced and I expect an answer by the end of the night."

"What makes you even want to go to Raven's house anyway?" Ms. Gladstone asks.

"Amina always spoke so highly of him so I decided that his house would be the best fit for my team."

Ms. Gladstone mumbles, "Even in death that broad is still fucking with your mind I see."

"I will not take your side remarks about the love of my life like that." Ms. Gladstone says, "Nomed, did you forget your place and think I am not free to say whatever the fuck I want to when it comes to you? You have no say so unless I want you to. The mere fact that I am having this conversation is strictly due to you serving my house. If not, I would have you on your knees right now."

"Forgive my outburst. I lost control of my emotions when Amina's name was spoken, but when can I expect an answer from your decision so I can inform Raven?" Nomed says. He tries to calm down between deep breaths as he stares at Ms. Gladstone.

"I will set up a meeting for Thursday to speak with the other noble houses. Also I will be going to speak to Raven so you don't have to speak with him at all. I will do it myself because if he is not offering me any of his commanders or generals I will not let any of you leave. So, to answer your little question, you can expect an answer from me in five days."

Nomed says, "Understood", and walks out of the room. He swiftly walks back to the room to talk to Gillie and Shelby. As he walks in, they both unanimously ask what Ms. Gladstone said.

"She said in two days she will be leaving and returning on Sunday. I will leave to go to see Demetri and Turan in order to finalize this attack and go over the plans. I will be back by the morning."

Nomed then heads to their secret lair in Canada. When he arrives, he opens the door and inside he sees Demetri and Turan have created a stone ping pong table and paddles and are having a very engaging game. As Turan spikes the rock they are using as a ping pong ball, Nomed catches it and says, "Hello boys. I hate to interrupt your game, but I have a favor to ask of you."

Demetri says, "So, are you finally going to let me out of this fucking prison?" Nomed smiles and says, "Yes, as a matter of fact, you guys do get to enjoy the outside world a little bit."

Turan then asks, "What is it that you want from us?"

"I want you guys to wear all black outfits and break into the Horens house and attack me. Make it seem like I am in danger and hopefully make Ms. Gladstone's son Jonathan run and unlock her secret room. As soon as he does I'm sure he will alert his mom and she will fly back as soon as possible. In the meantime, I will act like I have defeated the intruders and get him to come out. Shelby will then put a shield around his head until he passes out so that I can see what is in the room.

Demetri and Turan look at Nomed like he is crazy as he continues to talk, "All of the years working for the Horens house I have never seen or heard about this room I must know what's in there. That is what I need from you guys. Also Demetri, you get the benefit of killing a guard or two, just don't kill them all. You know how you get. Turan, I wouldn't use any big flame techniques – probably just have your hands or feet be on fire, something of that nature. There is a plane here you guys can use come Thursday as soon as nightfall arrives so that we can execute this mission. So, are you in?"

Demetri and Turan look at each other and back at Nomed. Turan speaks up first, "I think I speak for both of us when I say you are one crazy ass dude, Nomed; but, I also know that once you have a plan, you won't stop until it's fully executed. If you need us, we'll help you out."

Nomed smiles and gets up to walk out the door. He looks back and says, "Also Demetri no drinking on Thursday. I don't want you trying to kill me for real while we fake this attack."

When he gets back home, Nomed just sits and thinks about what all could go wrong, *"what if Jonathan doesn't open the door, what if he doesn't let me in, what if Ms. Gladstone comes back early, what if someone backs out?"* As Nomed starts to question his decision, he looks down at Amina's ring on his chain and says to himself, *"she would want me to do this,"* and immediately his resolve is concrete once again.

As he pulls up to the Horens noble house it just seems like a different place. As he walks into the room where Gillie and Shelby are, he says, "Everything is a go. All I need to know now is are you guys with me?"
Gilllie and Shelby both say, "We are with you no matter what."

As Wednesday morning comes along, Nomed is all smiles just thinking about the plan he has made up all by himself. In mid smile, Jonathan walks up to him and asks, "What are you so happy about today?"
"Don't you have a game today? I'm excited about that of course! I can't wait to see you play," Nomed says.

Nomed then gets up and starts to walk around the house, looking at every detail so that he doesn't forget anything. As he walks past Ms. Gladstone's office, she looks at Nomed and tells him to come into the office and shut the door behind him.

"After my trip, no matter what they decide Nomed, you will no longer be around my son. I don't want him around someone that is willing to leave my house and be disloyal. Now get the fuck out of my office."

Nomed politely gets up, scoffs and tells her, "You make sure to tell him that yourself," as he walks out the office. As he does, Ms. Gladstone slams down her bottle of whiskey.

That night, Nomed doesn't speak to anyone. He just sits in the middle of the mansion staring into space rambling through all of his thoughts about what must be done tomorrow. He barely gets any rest, but he is pumping with so much adrenaline that it doesn't even matter.

As daylight breaks, Jonathan comes down stairs and tells Nomed his mom said he can't hang with him anymore after her trip. He states that he tried to argue with her but it was to no avail and that she had already made up her mind.

Nomed grabs him and pulls him in for a hug and says, "This is all my fault. Don't you be sad about this. I will make sure that I stay in touch with you no matter what."

As they stand there, Ms. Gladstone walks pass them with her security detail and tells Nomed she will be back Sunday. The entire day, Nomed, Gillie, Shelby and Jonathan just sit around playing board games and video games. They are having a great time laughing, eating and fellowshipping together.

As the night begins to come, Nomed makes sure to call Turan and tell him to remind Demetri not to go crazy and to make sure not to kill Jonathan.

As nightfall is finally upon them, they are all listening to music and talking about Jonathan's last game when all of a sudden they hear gun shots.

"What's going on out there?" Jonathan yells.

"We will go check it out. Jonathan I need you to go to the secret place that your mom has set up for you. Take the back way just in case so no one sees you."

As Nomed finished that statement, the front door busts open. Wood chips from the now broken door are flying everywhere and they see two figures in all black. One, who punches the door into small pieces, and the other who has fists and feet made out of fire. They lay eyes on Nomed and his team and the bigger one of the two says, "Let's get rid of these vampires and take the boy for ransom as we discussed."

The smaller intruder grabs a piece of wood, sets it on fire and hurls it towards them. Shelby stops it with her shield. As the bigger one charges towards Jonathan, Nomed stops him, punches him to the ground and yells at Jonathan, "GO!!! I will come get you when I finish this. Don't open the door for anyone else and also call your mom and tell her what's going on."

At that moment he snaps out of shock and begins to run as fast as he can to his hiding place as Nomed told him. Jonathan is running as fast as he can across the property's land, constantly looking back to make sure no one is behind him. He can also see explosions going off all throughout the house.

Everything seems to be moving at the speed of light as Jonathan runs towards the fountain. As he reaches it, he stumbles, falling into the water. He gets up frantically and grabs the angel wing. The secret door opens up and he runs downstairs and gets to the door that leads to the safe room. As Jonathan gets to the door he places his thumb on the scanner and he places his eyeball so that it can be scanned. Ten rows of metal doors open up and between each one you can see guns and artificial sun rays. A voice says, *"Welcome Jonathan,"* and he begins to run in as the doors start to close behind him.

As he walks in, there's a huge table with at least twenty chairs around it and a computer screen with several different other screens attached to it. Once he walks closer to the screen, it turns on. He nervously pats himself trying to find his phone. He finally finds it and speed dials his mom. As she picks up he is talking fast and stuttering.

Ms. Gladstone yells and says, "Jonathan get a hold of yourself and tell me what the hell is going on! Just slow down son and let me know what's happening." Jonathan takes a deep breath and begins to tell his mom that the house has been attacked by two vampires and Nomed and his team have confronted them and that Nomed told him to go hide and that he will come find him when the intruders are gone.
"I'm sure Nomed will handle the intruders. I will call him to see if I need to rush home."

She hangs up and immediately calls Nomed, who on his end is trying to sound winded as he answers the phone.

"I'm a little busy at the moment, Ms. Gladstone," Nomed says. He points at Demetri to break something and Demetri obliges and punches a wall. All Ms. Gladstone can hear is a big boom and she asks, "Nomed do you have this taken care of or do I need to come back?"

"No ma'am. I will have these intruders eliminated for you in no time."

She tells Nomed to leave them alive so that she can deal with them when she gets back. Ms. Gladstone then tells Nomed Jonathan is safe and to call her when he has taken care of everything. She then hangs up and calls her son back. As he answers the phone, she tells him that Nomed will be taking care of everything shortly and that until he hears from her do not leave the room and most of all do not let any vampires in the room.

"It is important that no vampires ever walk in," she says.

"Yes ma'am," he says and hangs up the phone.

Meanwhile Nomed, Shelby, Gillie, Turan and Demetri are all sitting in the house laughing and drinking a celebratory shot of whiskey while thinking about how this plan has actually worked out so far. After about 3 hours Nomed says, "Finally I can go get Jonathan. Shelby, be ready and you other guys just be up there ready to act if I need you. Also don't forget to keep quiet while I call Ms. Gladstone."

Nomed picks up the phone and calls Ms. Gladstone. She picks up on the first ring.

"So is it finished?" she asks.

"Yes ma'am, I got rid of the intruders. I will try to find Jonathan and make sure he is okay."

"Jonathan will find you. He is totally fine. I will call him."

Nomed hangs up the phone and looks back at the team and says, "Let's move quickly."

In the meantime, Ms. Gladstone calls Jonathan and tells him that Nomed has taken care of the intruders and that he could leave the room.

"Are you sure there aren't any more vampires lurking around that could kill me?!"

"Of course I'm sure! Nomed told me himself. He also said that he will be coming to find you, so I need you out of that room so that nobody knows where it is."

"Yes ma'am," Jonathan says and hangs up the phone. Jonathan knows his mother said to leave the room, but he has no intention of moving until Nomed comes to get him.

Nomed receives another phone call with Ms. Gladstone yelling. "Are you sure there aren't any more intruders? Jonathan will be out on the land by himself." Nomed reassures her that Jonathan will be okay and that they will be to him in no time.

As they reach the fountain, Nomed tells everyone to stay up top and for Shelby to follow him down but to stay on the stairs so that Jonathan doesn't see her. As Nomed approaches the door, he begins to yell for Jonathan. "JONATHAN!!!! Jonathan, where are you?" Jonathan sees him in the camera standing in the hallway and jumps up in excitement.

He rushes to open the door for Nomed and deactivates the sun beams and guns. He runs to embrace Nomed. As he does, Nomed asked him if he was okay. Jonathan is silent and can't answer because Shelby has already put a shield over his face. All Jonathan sees is Nomed yelling and looking frantic before he passes out.

CHAPTER 7
"The Truth"

As Jonathan passes out, Nomed grabs him and throws him over his shoulder and yells for everyone else to come down. Everyone sits looking down the ten metal doors, sun beams, and guns in amazement.

Turan walks up and says, "Okay, I'll be the person to say it: it's clear that she didn't want you guys anywhere near this room," Turan walks around admiring the guns, "I wonder what kind of ammunition is even in these guns."
"Well thanks to Jonathan we are in so let's go," Nomed replies.

As they walk in, Nomed places Jonathan's body on top of the table. Gillie looks around and says, "The only thing in this room is a computer. Why would she want us not to touch these computers?"
"Well I guess we will find out," Nomed says as he sits down in front of it. He takes a deep breath, then taps enter on the on the keyboard.

The computer says, *"place thumb on validation pad."* Nomed looks back and tells Demetri to bring Jonathan over so that they can scan in his thumbprint. Then the computer asks for retinal validation and they hold open his eyelids so as the scan is complete. Demetri tosses him like a rag doll back onto the table. Nomed looks at him and says, "I told you not to harm him Demetri. Don't make me repeat that."

The computer opens up and there are several files on the desktop. Turan jokingly says, "This might take a while. We may need to have Demetri knock out Jonathan when he wakes up." Nomed then gives Turan the nastiest look of all time.
"That's not the slightest bit funny, so shut up," as he tries to decide which file to open first. Nomed then stumbles across a file named 'Dracula'. He clicks on it and it has three videos in it. Nomed clicks on the first video and it shows how the Nobles sent a squadron of people to Dracula's birth place and it goes into detail about what they learned from the writing on the walls. Also, the video talks about how the Nobles found out how to control all of the vampires.

The next the video shows how the Nobles collected blood on all vampires and they have it saved in different amulets that they carry around on them at all times. The video then goes on to show Dracula as he arrived at the noble house as called, and as he prepared to disappear he heard *'alon tatarus demon'* and was instantly frozen like a statute. You could tell the room was shaking because all of the cameras were not focused. As the nobles walked up to Dracula they made him tell them everything about the Bloodlust Four and how to control all vampires. Then after they took all the information they wanted, they told him to go to sleep until they asked him to awake.

The video ends and Shelby says, "So that is how they gained power over us."

Nomed then clicks on the next movie. It showed the second headmaster of the Horens house walking up to Dracula, waking him and making him have sex over and over with multiple women. The doctor documents that they are trying to make the ultimate vampire watch over the house of Horens, but are having issues with the host actually being able to carry the demon baby without dying and in turn, killing the vampire trying to grow inside of them. The doctor believes that no woman would be able to finish the birthing process.

Nomed then clicks resume on the video, it shows where a female subject has been put into a drug-induced coma after being impregnated and in turn, the baby growing inside of her is able to feed off of her and actually be born.

Turan looks at the video puzzled, whispering to himself, "What kind of freaky shit has been going on here?"

Nomed then sees a folder labeled *Demon'* and he clicks on it. On the screen, it reads *"Demon aka Nomed"* and his mouth drops along with everyone else's. As the video goes on, Nomed starts to see pictures of a child that is growing rapidly. Shelby walks up and says, "Nomed that little boy looks just like you." As the slide show keeps going a doctor's voice begins narrating what is going on in the pictures.

"Dracula's demon son, Nomed, has been growing at an increasingly fast rate. It seems in a full year he will probably reach the height of his growth and be a full adult."

It then starts to show pictures of Nomed as he looks now and it shows him going through several tests. Once again, the doctor begins speaking, "Just like his father, he doesn't have one particular power. He can learn powers as well. He is truly the perfect tool to have for the Horens house."

Gillie then says, "Before Turan says it I'm going to go ahead and say it. I'm completely mind-fucked."

Demetri chimes in and says, "Well, all that makes sense because you are too powerful to be a newborn vampire. I've only met a few vampires that aren't the kings that can knock me out."

"So I'm the son of Dracula," Nomed says, in pure shock, "I wonder if it says where they hid him."

As Nomed goes through the rest of the files, he sees a folder that says *'prized fighters'*. As he clicks on it, a list of all the fighters comes up: Nomed, Shelby, Gillie, Demetri, Leo, Arnoldo, Calderon, Braden, and Turan. Beside it, there is a list of commands: change incantation, terminate, and set free. Nomed then clicks on the incantation and it asks for a thumb print in order to work. He looks back at Jonathan and says, "I'll come back to this."

He then sees a folder that says 'completed missions'. At first he doesn't think that anything will be in there, but then he sees a folder that says 'Amina' and he clicks on it. A voice recording comes up of the phone call between Ms. Gladstone and Raven where she says that Amina has to be eliminated in order to keep Nomed at the Horens house. Next it goes to a video where they made Tunstall and Tala kill Amina.

As Nomed sits there and watches her last minutes everyone in the room notices that Nomed is about to blow. He turns around and noticed that Jonathan is up and has started crying. He watched the entire video as well. As Nomed sees Jonathan he snaps and dashes towards him and grabs him by the neck and begins to strangle him and says, "I will make her feel the same pain I did!!"
Shelby walks up to Nomed and says, "We still need him." Nomed looks back and then looks back at Jonathan and knocks him out.

Demetri laughs and says, "I'm just glad it wasn't me this time." Nomed is filled with rage at this point. In order to avoid killing Jonathan, he breaks the table in half and Jonathan's body slides down with it. "I can't believe she took the one thing I loved in this world! She will pay for this transgression against me!" Nomed yells.

Gillie looks back at the computer, "So this incantation part with all our names it, let's go back to that before you start destroying things." Gillie then walks up to the computer and goes to the file and clicks incantation and to his surprise, it gives them the option to change the incantation along with locking it so that no one else can change it. Gillie clicks on the incantation and changes it from *'alon tatarus demon'* to *'demons freedom movement'* and hits enter. An error message pops up and says 'Horens thumb'. Gillie turns around and everyone is looking at him. Turan steps forward and says, "You couldn't think of a better code?" Everyone shakes their head in disagreement, Gillie then says. "Okay guys, hear me out. It's so simple that people won't think that it's the password and plus, if

Nomed really plans on killing everyone nobody will know what our incantations are anyway or be able to change it. We can move this computer to our base in Canada so that they can't take anything off the hard drives and also, we would need to burn the Horens bodies just to make sure no one would be able to get their eyeballs or thumbprints. So, long story short, just bring the little boy over here."

They take Jonathan and pull him over to the computer. As they place his thumb over the scanner, Nomed says, "With our freedom we will take back what is rightfully ours. I trust all of you in this room, but it will take more than just us to complete the missions I have in mind. We will need all the prized vampires. Shelby, get Braden and Calderon here and Gillie could you get Demetri old team members Leo and Arnoldo here as well? Just tell them we have a major issue that must be handled ASAP."

With that Shelby and Gillie shake their heads and take out their phones. Shelby hangs up the phone and says they will be here before morning. Gillie hangs up and says, "I believe Arnoldo said him and Leo were going to race here so they should be here within the hour or so."

Meanwhile, as Jonathan wakes up, he is below the house in one of the prisoner cells and Nomed is standing looking at him. He immediately looks at Nomed and demands that he releases him. Nomed starts to laugh and says, "You are not in a position to boss me around as you please anymore. We got into that little safety room your mom had all of her dirty secrets stored away in."

"What does that have to do with me? Am I to pay for my mother's slight against you?" Jonathan asked.

"She took the one thing I loved away from me and I plan to do the same to her. Plus, I've learned a valuable lesson: don't leave people alive that envy you because they will find a way to turn on you. So the answer to your question is yes you will be the martyr of my cause. I hope you understand this was never my decision but your mom left me no choice."

Nomed turns and walks out and all you can hear are echoes of Jonathan yelling, "No come back! Come back! Don't leave me here Nomed! Don't kill me!" As Nomed walks out the room, he feels a tear roll down his face. Shelby catches this moment and says, "Are you sure you want to kill him? I know you have created a liking to him."

"Killing him will solidify me giving up the last piece of my humanity and starting my journey to become a vampire king."

As Nomed and Shelby proceed to walk upstairs, they hear what seems to be horses coming towards the house. They rush upstairs to see Gillie, Turan, and Demetri ready for a fight. All of a sudden they see two figures, one massive super human like image and a small slender one as well and Demetri says, "Guys it's alright, that's just Arnoldo and Leo."

As they walk in, Arnoldo has to lean under the door due to his massive size. Leo walks in behind him saying, "We rushed here thinking you guys needed help, but it seems you already took care of the invaders." They finally pay attention and look at the vampires in the room and notice Demetri is there and they are suddenly filled with joy as they go hug him and ruffle his hair.

"That's enough Arnoldo! I always feel like your little brother when you treat me like that."

DEMETRI

ARNOLDO

Leo looks at Nomed and says, "I guess I no longer have to worry about being blackballed for killing you against my master's wishes. I thought your story of not killing them was a joke."
"You no longer have to worry about being anyone's master, Leo. I have freed you guys so you are no longer bound by our previous masters. I will explain that story when the others get here, but in the meantime, let's repair this house so that we don't have to worry about the sunlight raining down on us and making this reunion really short."

Everyone begins to start rebuilding the parts of the house that are broken. During the clean-up Arnoldo walks over to Demetri and says, "I'm relieved you are alive. I've been meaning to ask you if you want to become my apprentice? I'm sure my training would teach you how to control that anger. What do you say?"

"Then you must know why I must decline that offer. I haven't forgotten how your master embarrassed me," Demetri says.

Leo walks by, overhearing what Demetri said and says, "A man who holds onto a grudge will eventually get lost in it. Remember that."
Demetri starts laughing, "Some things never change. Leo still has a quote for everything."

In no time, the group has finished all of the repairs on the mansion, and a few hours before daybreak Calderon and Braden come down from the roof and they see everyone already sitting in the main room.

Before anyone could speak, Braden says, "You guys don't even have to tell me, I already know. I've read Gillie's thoughts because he is not good at hiding anything."
Calderon then looks at Braden and says, "First of all, aren't you going to clue me in on what they're thinking, and second of all, how the fuck is Turan alive? I saw him die!"

Braden answers, "The deaths were real, but Gillie used his powers to reverse the time after they had proof that Demetri and Turan had been eliminated and after that fact they went and hid them in their secret base. As for your initial question, I will let Nomed answer that for you."

Nomed steps up to the bottom of the stairwell and says to Calderon, "I plan on killing Ms. Gladstone because she put out an order to have Amina killed. This all started when I asked her if I could leave and go be with Amina instead of being stuck to serve her. She felt like Amina was getting in the way, so she had her killed. Now, she must suffer the same fate."

"Nomed that is the stupidest shit I've heard in a long time," Calderon says, "You act like they don't have control over all of us! Would you even be able to stand to kill her?"

Nomed begins to laugh and says, "Well, what I didn't mention is that I freed you all and that you no longer belong to anyone. You are free vampires."

"How do we just automatically believe that you have freed us?" Calderon says skeptically.

Nomed immediately rushes upstairs to Calderon, while Braden simultaneously steps from behind so that he doesn't get caught in the crossfire. Nomed comes right beside him, scratches him and kicks him from the top of the stairs. Calderon slams into the table between all of the other prized vampires. As he crashes into it, the table breaks into pieces. Calderon wipes his blood from the scratch Nomed gave him and immediately grabs one of his elements off of his pants.

Meanwhile, Shelby puts a shield only around her, Nomed and Calderon. As Calderon set forth a fiery mini tornado, Nomed says, "Will you believe me now?" He holds up his hand, which has Calderon's blood all over it and says, *'demons freedom movement.'* Calderon instantly freezes up and Nomed commands him to disperse his powers. You can see the tension in Calderon face as he is struggling not to obey Nomed's orders.

A few seconds later, Calderon gives in to Nomed's powers and puts out the tornado. To add insult to injury, Nomed says, "Now, kneel to me as your new king." Calderon then kneels down and bows his head. Nomed lets him sit there for a few minutes, until which time Calderon then says, "You have made your point, Nomed. Could you let me up now?"

After a little thought, Nomed says, "Of course. You are released" and Calderon gets up. His face is red from trying to fight Nomed's wishes when asked to kneel. Calderon then goes and walks over to the bar and sits down and says, "Well I guess I have no choice but to be down for this rebellion."

Leo speaks for both he and Arnoldo, "All we saw was you hold up your hand and after that your voice came back and you control

Calderon. How are we supposed to believe that you actually have power over us?"

"You didn't hear anything until then because I didn't want you to hear. The incantation is a secret to you for now, because if you are not down with killing the Gladstones and are not fully in to support Nomed becoming the vampire king and killing all the old ones, we can't let you know how to free yourself," Shelby says.

Nomed walks down the stairs with Braden and says, "We didn't let you know the words because if you are not with us, you are free to leave without us touching a hair on your head, but if you hear the incantation, there's no way we would let either of you leave alive if you were not going to go along with the plan."

Leo and Arnoldo look at each other and shake their heads. Arnoldo then says, "We are with you, but you can't blame us for not believing in freedom when we have been slaves for so long."

Next Nomed looks at Braden and says, "Well, what's your decision? I know you already know the incantation because of Gillie's thoughts."

Braden looks at Nomed and says, "As long as Shelby is with you I'm willing to follow you to the end of the world."

"Well, I guess it has been settled then."

Nomed then orders everyone to give a sample of blood as an insurance and failsafe. After everyone has given a small drop he asks Calderon if he could create a hard ring out of the blood and Calderon says it would be no problem and that the task would be easy. As Calderon brings the blood out of the capsule, he mends it with a metal that he had on him and then give Nomed the ring. Nomed then takes off his necklace and puts the ring right by the charm he got Amina.

He sits down in the chair and says, "Ms. Gladstone will be back Sunday night. I plan on having her entire team killed and I want to drain her son of all of the blood he has in his body, then I will kill her."

"But Nomed, you have never drank blood before," Gillie says. "I'm no longer going to hide what I am, Gillie. We were born of blood and from now on I will take it from those who oppose me and in turn every noble family member and security guard I want you guys to drink their blood as well."

Demetri chimes in, "For all of you who have been a prized vampire and never drank blood before be advised: your powers may mutate or fully blossom."

Gillie says, "You say that like it's a bad thing. Should we be concerned? I may not mind having enhanced powers."

"You don't know the thirst that comes along with the pure thrill of having real blood run through your body. As you can see, I can't even control my bloodlust. What if one of you become the same way?" Demetri says.

Nomed says, "There is no need to control our urges any longer. There will be a lot of blood ahead of us and we don't need anything holding us back."

Arnoldo looks at Demetri and adds, "Just become my pupil so that I can teach you how to control that. Just like I can teach anyone who follows in your footsteps as well."

Demetri slams his hand down on his chair, "That is never going to happen, Arnoldo. Let it go!"

"Guys, guys! What is the deal? Just so I can be clear, what is the beef between you two? Did he lose a fight to you, Arnoldo?"

"No, he lost a fight to my maker, Prime. I am the reason behind Demetri only having those scars instead of not having his life. Prime was going to kill him and deep down I really think that's what Demetri wanted him to do. Ever since I stopped them he has held a grudge with me," Arnoldo confessed.

"Who is Prime? I've never heard of him," Nomed inquired.

"Prime was the person that taught me muscle manipulation and you haven't heard of him because he is no longer around thanks to a snitch. So the real reason I'm joining you is to repay my master's death by finding that person. He is in Norie's vampire house, so as long as I can kill him I'll kneel to you as king."

Leo then says, "We need to have a plan in order for this to work, and also I don't feel comfortable with going into battle not fully knowing all of your abilities and weaknesses."

"I'm glad you said it before I did," Braden said. "I'm sorry, but in order to take both the noble house and vampires' house down we are going to need to know who does and does not need to be stuck with each other just in case we get separated."

Nomed says, "Fine. I'll start." Nomed started, "I just found out that I am Dracula's son. Due to my father's abilities, I really don't have many vulnerabilities. I have super strength, fire doesn't bother me, and I have fast speed and sometimes I take powers from some of the other vampires. I fight and I always wondered why around certain vampires when they use their powers, I feel like I've had them before. It finally makes some sense why I feel that way."

Leo then says, "But Dracula didn't have a kid before he disappeared."

Nomed explains what information he found, "The Nobles have been hiding Dracula away from everyone so that he could never be freed. At the same time, they have been running experiments on him. That pretty much sums up all of the power I have."

Gillie then steps up and says, "I am a time-shifter. I can move back time at my own pleasure. The only problem is if I reverse someone from being killed, I can't use that ability for three days. Also, if I keep someone from being killed and if they get killed again like I said there's nothing I can do."

Calderon asks, "So why do you carry around those weird shaped guns? I have never seen you use them."

Gillie then pulls out a gun and shoots it towards the wall. A black lightning bolt hits the wall and Gillie then makes the black bolt go back into his gun.

"So why is it a lightning bolt and what element is that?" Calderon asks.

"I don't know I just like the lightning bolt and I have no idea what kind of element it is. All I know is when I go back in time, this little black water like material is all around but only I can see. So I've just been collecting it and realized through a minor altercation that I can actually use it as I want."

Calderon immediately says, "What do I have to do in order for you to give me some?"

"You've already pledged allegiance to my best friend, so it's free for you," Gillie says.

Shelby then walks up and says, "Now that Calderon is finished finding out a way to add a new element to his arsenal, my powers are simple. I can create a shield that's highly powerful. It can let us talk without being heard, and I can also let us all walk in the sun for fifteen minutes. My main downfall is that's all I can do. I don't really have any other amazing powers."

She then looks over at Leo and says, "So, what's your deal?"

Leo says, "Well since you asked, I am a master swordsman. To be more exact, I can wield any weapon I choose but I prefer swords. I also have an heightened IQ. It's hard for me not to go through every scenario before I enter a situation. Also, I have enhanced speed, agility, and strength. My downfall, if I had to pick something, is maybe that I can't fly and I always wanted to fly. With that, I will give the stage over to Arnoldo."

As Arnoldo stands, everyone realizes how much of a behemoth he is. His giant stature has everyone wondering if he is even a vampire Nomed says, "Before you start, why are you so much bigger than normal vampires?"
"My maker, Prime, was showing me the techniques of muscle manipulation and by going through the process you can't help but grow in size by putting extraordinary strain on your body. My muscles remember the pain and grow. Nobody knows but earthquakes, tornados, and tsunami are the causes of my training so I can't go all out like I would like to because I would destroy the regions of the world. I have super strength. I can move mountains if I wish and all of my body is about 60% shy of being pure muscle. My downfall is with my size, it sometimes creates problems fighting smaller opponents because they get into my blind spots."

Demetri butts in and says, "And you want to be my mentor."
"At least I don't go into a blind rage when I fight Demetri. You are just good at fighting and that's it. Your major downfall is that you can't stop focusing on bloodshed to be useful during a fight unless Turan is around."

Demetri then sits down and says, "Well I guess I don't need to go. It's your turn Braden."

Braden steps forward and says, "I am the strongest telepath and telekinetic wielding vampire in the world. As far as weaknesses, I would probably have to say it's been ages since I've actually been in a fight where I've had to actually try and win." He then says, "Well Calderon, it's on you."

Calderon steps up and says, "I'm an elemental. As long as an element is around me I can use it as my weapon and I even carry elements around with me in order to never be without one. My downfall would have to be the fact that I'm young and I haven't faced many battles...yeah that would have to be it."

Turan steps up and says, "I'm glad you saved the best for last. I can control all flames. My major downfall is water, duh! I don't think I have to describe that one to you guys, huh?" Everyone starts to laugh and then in unison they agree that fire and water don't mix.

As they all sit around, Nomed says, "Do whatever you want to this night because after tomorrow night we will be in an all-out war." He gets up and walks to the safe room.

As he gets into the room, he sits down in the chair and he finds the folder that has Amina's death footage in it. He opens the file and presses play. As he sit and watches Tunstall and Tala as they let Amina send out her message, the tears roll down his face.
He watches them kill her as peacefully as they can. Even afterwards, they put all of her stuff by her body before they left.

Out of nowhere, the screen goes blank. Nomed turns around and Shelby leans over and hugs him. He looks over and he realizes Gillie had unplugged the computer.
"Did your dumbass really think you were going to sit and watch this movie the entire time? Come with us, Shelby will put up a shield. We are moving this computer as soon as night falls."
Nomed is slow to move and Gillie pushes him along, "Let's go, Nomed. This is not a time for tears. This is a time for retribution! Let go of sorrow and emotion and give into hate and destruction because that is what we as a team are going to need from you."

Shelby wipes Nomed's face and tells him now is the time he needs to be strong for Amina and destroy anyone who opposes them.

Next, Shelby puts a shield around them and they speed towards the house. As they walk in, they realize everyone is still in the room preparing their minds for what is about to happen.
Nomed says, "Why didn't you guys take some of the secret passages to go out?"
Leo says, "We all have talked and we are a little bit excited so we don't want to mistakenly miss the fight."

Nomed just shrugs and says, "I feel the same way. Can't really get my mind off what's to come, but I am going upstairs to get some rest. I advise you guys to do the same. Tonight will be a long one."

CHAPTER 8
"Vengeance"

Nomed is awakened by Ms. Gladstone calling. He picks up the phone and she tells him she has tried to reach Jonathan the last couple of hours and he has not answered.

"I'm sorry, Ms. Gladstone. I meant to tell you. His phone was broken during the attack on the house. I offered to take him to get one but he said he would rather wait until you get here and buy another one." Nomed then says, "Do you want me to go get him so that you can speak with him? I believe he is on the basketball court shooting around"

Ms. Gladstone then replies, "No it's fine. I'll just see him when I get there tonight. I was just worried because I hadn't heard from him in so long and I just wanted to reach out and make sure that he was okay."

"No need to fear, he is in great hands. Just curious though, what did the council say about me and my team leaving to be with Raven's vampire house?" Nomed said.

Ms. Gladstone says, "I was hoping to give you this information face to face but since you asked I guess I will tell you now. Everyone voted against you going to Raven's house because it would make the houses unbalanced. Raven's vampire house would have the strongest vampires in the world and that would lead to there being a great imbalance in power."

Nomed begins to laugh, "I would expect nothing less from the lot of you. I knew my simple wish would not be granted."

Ms. Gladstone interrupts and says, "Nomed I understand why you're mad, but you have to believe that I fought to the ends for you and your team to leave."

"Yes, that is true. You have always had my best interest in mind, right?" Nomed said sarcastically.

"Of course! I always have put you first when it comes to making you happy."

Nomed then replies, "I will make sure to repay you with the same kind of happiness soon. I'll just see you when you get here, boss" and hangs up. He decides to get up and see what everyone else is doing. It seems they all had fallen asleep over in the same room he left them in. Nomed realizes it's several boxes of pizza everywhere. "Hey you guys, when did you order pizza?" Nomed said shockingly. Shelby looked up and said, "Yeah I went to the door and grabbed it really fast," she laughed.

Nomed laughs and says, "That makes sense." He grabs a box and a soda out of the fridge and he walks towards the door that leads to the prison cells.

Gillie yells out, "You really like this kid, huh?"

Nomed turns around and says, "Fuck off, Gillie," and slams the door behind him.

As he walks down the stairs, he hears Jonathan yell, "Who is that? Who is coming?!" As Nomed walks around the corner, he says, "Oh, it's just the vampire jackass. What are you doing here and what do you want? I thought we were friends, Nomed! You are nothing more than a ruthless vampire."

"I understand that you are mad but your mom brought this upon you and if I was really not your friend I wouldn't bring you your favorite meal: pepperoni pizza. I even brought soda, which your mom doesn't let you drink, so I believe I'm being highly nice considering the circumstances because I could bring you water or nothing at all and have you starve until she makes it back tonight."

Nomed goes on to say, "Either way it goes, I just hope you forgive me for what's going to happen tonight. You have really became one of the people that I thought about needing to protect for their entire lifetime. I have been battling myself for this entire time on if I should kill you or not, but one thing is clear: blood must be paid in blood. I can't make my first stance as a leader by going back on my word. I have to do this to remove myself from caring about your family – by killing the person I care about the most first.

Jonathan then replies, "Well at least me knowing you care about me makes my upcoming death a little more bearable. I'll make sure not to cry or yell. I guess we all do have to pay for the sins of our fathers and mothers. Am I right, Nomed? So how will you pay for your father's sins after tonight?"

"I can tell you are your mother's son. You have accepted your fate and ran head first into it. To answer your question, I've never known my father, so I can only better my life and run it how I feel. Also, since I'm such a nice guy I even brought you some whiskey so we can have your first drink. No man should die before having a good drink or two."

Jonathan just begins to laugh and says, "I thought for sure I was going to live longer or at least make it into my twenties, so I guess a drink or two won't kill me."

As they sit down in the basement and laugh, the time seems to go slowly by as they reminisce on what times they did share together.

As the bottle of whiskey slowly starts to disappear, Nomed strengthens his resolve and tells Jonathan, "See you later kid." He walks back up the stairs, never looking back at Jonathan. Despite knowing what had to be done, somewhere in the back of his mind, he made a friend in Jonathan and he didn't want to see him go. As he walks upstairs, everyone is waiting for him. Gillie says he already called Ms. Gladstone and that she should be there in three hours.

"So what's the plan Nomed?"

"Ms. Gladstone always traveled with about sixty armed soldiers, her family council, and usually she would have us with her so she will have no vampires we have to worry about. Leo, Turan, and Demetri: you guys attack the back of the convoy or cars. Braden, Arnoldo, Calderon: you guys attack the middle and syphon in everyone else. Shelby and Gillie, we all know she will have six body guards with her, so I need you guys to take care of them and leave Ms. Gladstone to me. I don't want a hair touched on her head until she loses everything she cares about and feels the pain I did."

As nightfall comes, Nomed tells Leo, Turan, and Demetri to go outside to the front gates so that they can make sure that all of us are behind them as they park. Calderon, Arnoldo, and Braden will stay by the house so that as soon as they attack the back cars, they could surprise the middle cars and above everything else make sure to call Nomed as soon as they came through the gate, and then everyone scatters out the house towards their designated positions.

As everyone sits, sweating and full of nervousness like they haven't completed thousands of missions, Nomed rushed out to Braden and says, "It just hit me! I forgot you can link all our minds! Do that so we can communicate freely."

Braden links everyone's thoughts and then Nomed says, "I know all of you are probably feeling how I am: anxious and nervous, but believe me, when this battle starts that feeling will quickly go away."

Leo then cuts in and says, "Nomed, we have about fifteen cars approaching the gates!"

The gates open and the entire convoy of cars come through the gate. Behind the cars, all you see are flashes from Demetri, Leo, and Turan. One of the drivers looks back and thinks that he saw something behind them and ask the guard next to him, "Did you see that?" The driver shrugs and continues to drive. As all the cars pull up, Ms. Gladstone rolls down the window and says, "You can't even tell that it was a fight here." All the cars park and the groups of troops and people get out of the cars. Nomed reminds everyone drink the blood of these humans, "We will no longer hold our kind to nectar."

Next thing you know, there is a blaze of fire around the cars. As Ms. Gladstone looks back, she sees Demetri and Leo slashing and ripping her soldiers apart. She grabs the amulet on her chest and yells *"alon tatarus demon."* Turan looks up at her as blood is dripping from one of the soldier's neck he is feeding on, smirks and he continues to feed.

At this point, Ms. Gladstone begins to panic. She looks closer and sees Arnoldo smash three of her cabinet members into the ground and Braden throwing people into the cars. Out of the corner of her eye, she sees Calderon moving the fire towards her. At this point, all you can hear are the screams of everyone around her. She calms herself and says, "Alpha squad on me!" and she starts to move towards the house. As they get close to the door, it opens and Gillie shoots a bolt that hits three of her squad members. He then grabs one by the throat and starts to drink his blood.

Next she looks to her right and all the rest of her squadron are reaching for their neck as if they can't breathe. Shelby comes out of nowhere and begins smashing in their skulls. Ms. Gladstone then runs into the house yelling Jonathan's name. When she gets into the main room, she sees Nomed holding Jonathan by the throat. She immediately yells, *"Alon tatarus demon!"*
Nomed starts to laugh, "That won't work on us anymore."

Ms. Gladstone asked in a panic, "Why are you doing this? Is it because we declined you leaving? Other than that one thing, I have been nothing but good to you, haven't I?!"
Nomed's face goes stale, "Nothing but good to me? Is that the reason you planned on never letting me stop serving you?"

"All you had to do was give me some time, I would have figured out a way to set you free. Was it not I that have counseled you and mentored you your entire life? I thought we were a family, Nomed!" Nomed then says, "If everything is true that you say and we are family, why did you have Amina killed knowing she was the love of my life?!"

Ms. Gladstone starts to laugh and says, "Nomed where did you get that outlandish idea from, I would never do that."

Nomed begins to scratch Jonathan's neck and blood starts to leak. He then says, "And still even faced with the truth you try to lie to me. It is over and the truth is out now. I got into that little room of yours with all of your dirty secrets. I've seen the tapes and rest assured you and the other noble houses and vampire kings will feel my pain. I'm going to make sure of that."

Ms. Gladstone says, "So I see the truth is out. You know what, Nomed? You are right. I couldn't let someone as powerful as you leave and be alone so I did what was best for us and had her eliminated."

Nomed yells, "Best for us?! No! It was best for you and now it's time for you to pay for your sins."

"Just let Jonathan go. He is like your brother. He has always looked up to you."

Nomed then says, "You are right. He has grown on me but he is just like you, so he already understands why he must die. There is no way you could save his life because you will die today. Tell me, where you have hidden my dad and I may let him live."

Ms. Gladstone says, "There's no way I'll tell you the location of that monster. Between the two of you guys, you could rule the world in less than a week."

Nomed says, "So be it" and he bites into Jonathan's neck and for the first time he tastes the warm blood. As it courses throughout his body, he feels himself automatically get stronger and he releases his bite while saying, "So this is what real blood does." He looks at Ms. Gladstone and says, "Last chance before it's over for him."

With tears in her eyes she says, "Even if I wanted to help, we had a vampire wipe our minds of where we took Dracula and had Raven kill that vampire. The only person that may know the location is Dr. Montauge. He knows everything and that's all I know. I promise."

Nomed then looks and says, "Everything you said still won't save him. I've learned from my foster mother that you only use people in order to get what you want and now that I know a name I can go ask him or kill him and go from there." Nomed goes on to say, "Now Ms. Gladstone, feel the same despair that I did." Nomed bites back into Jonathan's neck and begins to drain him. As the last bit of life flows from his body, Ms. Gladstone sees a sword on the wall, goes and grabs it and charges towards Nomed.

As Nomed drains Jonathan's body, he throws the corpse into the wall and takes the full force of Ms. Gladstone's blade through his stomach. As he grabs her by the neck, he pulls the sword out and flings it to the ground. Ms. Gladstone's feet dangle as she struggles for air.

"Now you can finally feel my pain. I have taken the most important thing from you, just like you did me. The truth is that it saddens me to have to be the one to do this because I honestly thought you cared about us, but it's clear that we are nothing more than tools to you. You should rest easy knowing that it was your actions for why the world will suffer."

Ms. Gladstone struggles to get air so that she can talk and when she does she looks at Nomed and says, "Get it over with you fucking bitch" and in that second she feels her body go numb as Nomed takes her heart out with his bare hands.

As he drops the body he mutters, "Now you can be as heartless as I am."

CHAPTER 9
"To Become King"

He holds his blood stained face up and realizes everyone is looking at him and they are covered in blood also.

Turan then walks up to Gillie and says, "Fuck!!! Here you go" and hands him a hundred dollars. As he looks at Nomed and says, "I really thought you weren't going to kill both of them but it was definitely worth me losing the money. You're a real savage bro. I'm pretty sure that was one of the best deaths I've seen in a while."

Nomed walks up and says, "You guys are assholes! Who bets on something like that?" They all burst out laughing and then Nomed says, "On a serious note, did drinking blood for the first time make you guys feel more powerful?"

Arnoldo interrupts and says, "I forgot a few of you haven't tasted human blood before, but yes, when you drink blood for the first time your powers mature so I'm sure you, Shelby, Gillie, Turan, and Calderon will see some drastic changes in your powers over the next few days."

Nomed says, "I figured as much. I could tell something was different, but I don't have this urge to feed like everyone said I would."

Arnoldo then says, "The nectar that they give you guys has some type of formula in it that lessens your urges to want blood. Just wait until that wears off; after not drinking blood. A lot of you newborns won't ever know that feeling because that nectar never really gets out your system, which is a gift in its own right, but time will tell who is immune and who is not. I can help anyone who struggles with that and make it disappear."

Nomed says, "That is great to know, but I hope none of us have that issue. We need to decide how we are going to take down Norie's vampire house. Are we going to just take down the front door powers blazing, or do we get invited in the house and then start the fight with their commanders? I do want to give a lot of them the option of not fighting and protecting the house when we are not there but I also know the captains, commanders, and top fighters we will have to kill or cripple."

Nomed looks towards Gillie, "I need you and Demetri to take that computer to our base in Canada and we need to make sure nobody ever finds it."

"I know a vampire that can make the entire base seem as if it's not there but he isn't cheap and he makes you feed him," Demetri says. Nomed looks and says, "Money is all around here. Make sure to pay the man. Just don't show him how you got to our hideout. We will have to keep him prisoner there. Let him know that he won't be able to leave as he would like, so take some of these movies and games there. Get plenty of blood or nectar, depending on whichever he likes to use."

Nomed looks Demetri in his eyes and says, "Make sure to tell him that this may take a while and I'm talking years." Demetri nods his head and says, "I got you, boss."

Demetri and Gillie leave and head to Nomed's team base in Canada. As everyone waits for them to return, Nomed asks Turan and Calderon to burn all of the bodies except Jonathan's.

Shelby says, "I knew you were going to do something special for him. Just remember wherever you bury his body that no one ever needs to be able to find it."

Nomed says, "I have the perfect place in mind. I'll be back later on tonight."

Nomed decided to bury Jonathan's body in Mexico at the Mayan ruins. As he gets to the location, he looks at Jonathan's body and says, "I'm sorry kid. You really were one of my best friends. Your death was the only way to pay Alice, well, I mean your mom, back." Nomed begins to laugh and says, "You know, that's the first time I've called her that in years. I've actually had a burden lifted off of my shoulders."

Nomed feels a tear roll down his cheek. Upon realizing that, he shifts his mood and says, "I will make sure that your death is not in vain. I will become the one and only vampire king and I will run a world where vampires are no longer slaves. It sucks that I can't put a marker on your grave but I know who you are and that's all that matters. Hell, who knows, I may see you on the other side." Nomed begins to laugh, "Who am I kidding? I'm pretty sure we won't be in the same place. I'll definitely have to fight my way through hell if I'm ever killed."

Just like that he turns and begins his trip back to the Horens house. When he arrives, he walks through the door and everyone is waiting on him.

Gillie walks up and says, "So what's our next move?"

Nomed says, "Well first, I'm going to kill Norie, but this will be our first all-out battle versus vampires. I'm sure most of the people at the house will leave when they see we are there for a fight. We just have to worry about his most loyal members. So I guess we can see who stays and pick which person we want to take on from there. Today we party and right after nightfall tomorrow, we will go to house Dracula and take down Norie."

Demetri starts to laugh and says, "This will be fun. Just promise me none of you guys will die tonight."

"I won't let that happen," Nomed says, "I'll make sure we all make it through this one. Now, everybody get some rest."

When everyone awakens, it's still daytime and Nomed is sitting in the living room just listening to music with a cup of liquor. He turns and says, "Now that everyone is up, let's get ready to head to house Dracula and take Norie's seat as a vampire king."

Leo says, "How are we going to get there? We usually race. Is that how you guys want to do it?"

Gillie comes in and says, "Absolutely not! We are going to take the plane and go from there."

Turan says, "I guess that was decided quickly. Good try though, Leo. If Nomed would have agreed to that we would have just met you guys there. I'm not into all that running and racing for no reason and I'm sure Gillie's lackadaisical self wasn't going to race either.

Gillie shrugs and says, "At least you guys know me already."

Shelby walks up and says, "Okay guys! Let's go to house Dracula. I'm ready to get this over with. I'm actually ready to get in a good fight."

The plane ride over is completely quiet other than Turan steadily snapping his fingers and creating a random light in the back of the plane until Calderon makes the flame explode in his face. Turan yells at the front of the plane, "Calderon! You are an asshole!"

He replies by saying, "I just did what everyone was thinking. I can't get into my zone with you back there trying to be a nightlight."

Nomed walks in the back and says, "Ok guys, we are here. I hope you are as excited as I am."

The plane lands and everybody walks off the plane. Nomed walks up to the gate and kicks it open. As the two pieces of the gates roll through the front yard, one hits a fountain and the other hits a tree. Arnoldo says, "Now that is the way you announce you have come to fight. I wonder if they got the message."
Nomed says, "I guess it's only one way to find out" and they begin to walk to the front door.

Gillie says, "Why are all the houses so far from the front gate? I feel like we have been walking for an hour, but at least we are almost there. Do you plan on kicking this door in as well?"

Nomed begins to laugh and says, "We have only been walking for two minutes and no I'm going to try to leave that door intact. We are going to take up residency in this house so I would like to keep it in good condition if possible. Before the fights begin, don't forget to try not to kill the strong vampires. Someone has to protect this house while we are away. However, if you have to kill them because they are too loyal to Norie, kill them without a second thought. I hope everyone understands that. Now let's go."

Nomed pushes open the door and they see dozens of vampires mingling, dancing, and partying. Nomed sees the DJ booth, walks over, jumps in the air and with both hands come crashing down breaking the entire booth. As the music stops, everyone is looking at them.

Nomed yells out to the crowd cockily, "If you don't want to die, leave this place until tomorrow because I am here to take Norie's spot as a vampire king!" Nobody moves. The biggest person he sees, Nomed decides to make an example out of him. He goes over and punches him through the wall and out the house. He turns around and says, "So, I'm assuming you guys are all our enemies." Meanwhile behind him, Leo takes out his swords, Calderon creates a small tornado, and Turan sets his whole body a blaze. The crowd begins to run out of the building. A voice then comes over the building and it says, "You really had the nerve to come into this place and demand my guests around like you own the place."

All the prized vampires turn around to see Norie and all his most powerful vampires.
"See the problem with you prized vampires is that you believe that you're the most gifted out of the prized vampires. Who do you think gave up a spot for you maggots to take the seat to shine? I'll let you

guys in on a little secret: every vampire house has their own set of exceptional vampires that were prized vampires at some point. Do you guys really believe that you can kill every one of them and possibly kill me afterwards? Ha! Don't fool yourself! Go back home before I tell Ms. Gladstone that you have gotten out your cage and likewise for you other prized vampires."

Nomed laughs and says, "You must be going to hell in order to find her and deliver that message."

"What do you mean? What the fuck have you done, you idiot?"

"We killed her and her entire family and body guards."

Norie looks at Nomed like he's lost his mind, "Do you know what they will do to you when they find you? They have a power over you guys that cannot be broken. You understand that, right?"

Nomed confidently says, "We are no longer worried about that. We are free from our shackles and there is no person or thing living that can change that. Speaking of, what kind of coward are you? Clearly you said they have us bound but that didn't sound like you were including yourself. Do you mean to tell me that you are not bound by that incantation and yet you haven't rebelled and found the person that created you?"

Norie interrupts and says, "How dare you question my loyalty! Of course I'm bound. Do you believe that someone who's as close to Dracula as me would not be on a leash?"

"I don't believe you," Nomed says.

Gillie interjects and says, "It's funny you say that, 'cause I saw Raven completely unphased by the incantation when Ms. Gladstone said it around us, after he and Nomed got into a fight."

Nomed looks back at Norie and says, "It seems like I don't need you to answer that then, so let's save this small talk for later. I'm here for your head. Let's move this outside. I don't want to mess up my new house."

Norie angrily shouts, "Everyone out!!! Butlers and servants don't return until morning. There is about to be a battle here that you guys wouldn't be able to help with even if you wanted to."

All of the servants that were left begin to leave the house and Norie reassures them that he will make tomorrow's party even bigger and better. As everyone leaves the house, Norie looks at Nomed and says, "This group of vampires is known for doing the impossible and as it seems the numbers of them to you are the exact same, so if you can't defeat them it's no point in you even trying to fight me. So, this was a nice little show, but I'll be in my sanctuary looking forward to see who comes in to greet me saying the job is done."

As he walks off Nomed's vampires and Norie's team try to size up each other. Nomed says, "Can we at least know the names of the people we are going to kill? Even though I already know I want to fight Mario."

Mario begins to laugh, "Well, I guess my name has already been told, or at least well known. Next to me is my older brother Markus. That's Maurice, Arma, Dunkan, Hoyt, Kali, Narkisa, and lastly Wynn. We also already know who we want to fight. We have been watching you guys for years on the TV so we already know what you guys are capable of, so let's get this started."

Norie's vampires waste no time, as Arma jumps up and immediately punches Arnoldo through the ground. Hoyt walks up to Braden and says, "How about we take a walk outside?" Maurice looks at Turan and says, "You and Nomed can stay right here. I think we will take care of you guys in no time." Kali then jumps from the balcony and disappears. Next thing you see is Shelby flying through one of the walls in the building. Gillie looks and says, "Did anyone catch that shit?"

Next thing you know, Markus swings a massive black scythe towards Gillie and as he leaps back Markus kicks him through the front doors and follows behind him. Narkisa begins to fight with Leo, Wynn creates a wind vortex and moves it towards Calderon who grabs it and is thrown into a tree. Demetri looks at Dunkan and says, "I hope you're strong because I'm usually the last person ready for a fight," and before Demetri can finish his sentence he is sent outside by a massive sounds wave. Dunkan then looks at Mario and Maurice and says, "We will be back. Just take care of those two," and leaps off the balcony and goes to find Demetri.

CHAPTER 10
"The Battles"

Arma vs. Arnoldo

As the smoke clears, Arnoldo realizes he has been punched down into one of the training facilities under the mansion. He looks and says, "Arma, isn't it? You sure do pack a massive punch, but it won't be anything that I can't handle," as Arnoldo wipes the blood from under his lip.

Arma walks up to Arnoldo and says, "Don't underestimate me because I've been sitting back, hoping people forget about the devastation my strength used to cause. We are no good for our master if everyone knows our powers and it's limits."
"So you guys have limits? That's cute," and he charges towards Arma and punches him in the face. Arma is lifted off his feet and Arnoldo grabs him by the face and slams him to the ground.

He begins to pummel him into the ground with a barrage of punches. As he is punching, he begins to hear laughing and he stops punching. As the smoke clears, he sees that now Arma has four arms.

Instantly, he is grabbed by his neck with the first pair of arms and is pulled close to Arma as he says, "I blocked all of those weak punches, but it was entertaining thinking that you were actually doing something. So let me shake you up a bit." The new pair of arms start hitting Arnoldo in the gut multiple times and finally he is hit hard with two right hooks to the face. His body flies over the hole he had just created by smashing Arma's body into the ground and his body hits the concrete and tumbles until his body comes to a stop.

As Arnoldo regains his composure, Arma says, "I guess I can let you in on my special ability. My body can create multiple arms, each set making me stronger and stronger than the set before. There is no way you can win this even with your monstrous strength."

Arnoldo then looks up and says, "You have watched me during my fights but you have no idea what I'm capable of. Today we will test those limits that you talked about earlier," and they both charge towards each other. Arnoldo is blocking all of Arma's punches and then he attacks back and sends Arma flying into the wall. Next thing you know, Arma has three pairs of arms now and he tells Arnoldo, "I see I can no longer play with you. It's time to crush you."

In a matter of seconds, he is in front of Arnoldo and he starts to punch him as if his fists were a machine gun. With blood flowing from his mouth, Arnoldo says, "You have earned the right to see me at my best," and Arnoldo drops his guard and his body is sent flying into the wall. Arnoldo pulls himself out and takes off his gloves. Arma begins to laugh and says, "I feel no power increase, so what was the point of you taking off your gloves?"

"Come at me and find out," Arnoldo says. Arma attacks him with all he had and Arnoldo is blocking every punch thrown his way. Arma realizes that Arnoldo's body is transforming with every hit that he absorbs. Arma stops and says, "What the hell are you?"

Arnoldo laughs and says, "Well since you asked, other than strength my main power is being able to adapt to the amount of force or pain I'm going through. My body adapts to that but it can only be done if my skin touches the person's skin. I try not to use this ability because I want to win battles with my own strength, but I always seem to find someone stronger than the mountain I've already ascended to."

Arma looks thrilled and says, "I see, but I'm sure that has its limits also, so I will push my limits in order to break yours."

Arma lets out a huge roar and grows a fourth set of arms. "With this my power is four times that of before."

Arnoldo looks and says, "At least I know your body can't grow anymore arms. I'm not even sure where you would put them, to be honest."

Arma charges and his attacks begin to push Arnoldo back and with all the looks of determination on his face, he finally pays attention to Arnoldo's face and realize that he is not breaking a sweat at all.

Arnoldo looks him in his eyes and says, "With this power of yours you could never defeat me. I am the one and only pupil of Prime. I would disgrace him if I was to lose to someone like you. Now you will feel my might!"

Arnoldo cocks his fist back and blue sparks of light start to flicker. He punches Arma in the stomach and blood goes everywhere and Arma falls to the ground. With blood coming out of his mouth, Arma says, "How is there such a great difference in our power? How did you do it?"

Arnoldo walks over to him and says, "How about I teach you? I've been looking for a pupil and we need someone to protect this house while we are not around. What do you think about my offer?" "I don't mind becoming your pupil, but I just want you to know once I achieve your power, I will challenge you again."
"Great! That was a good answer because if you said no I was going to separate your head from your body."

As Arnoldo turns around to walk off Arma yells to him, "Wait, why can't I move?"

Arnoldo says, "Oh yeah, I forgot to mention that. I punched a piece of your spine out. It will take a few days to grow back, but don't worry, I'll be back down here to get you after this battle has concluded. Until then just sit tight." Arnoldo smiles and keeps walking.

Arma begins to laugh also and says, "You're definitely an asshole. I think I picked the right master."

Hoyt vs. Braden

Hoyt and Braden seem to be having a casual stroll, trying to find a pleasant place to battle. As they are walking, Braden sees Demetri flying past him. Demetri yells, "Hey Braden, fancy meeting you here," as he continues to be carried away. They see Dunkan pass by them as well chasing after Demetri. Hoyt looks at Braden and says, "Look at the brutes. They only know how to destroy things."
"So I'm guessing you don't have super strength or speed, seeing that you picked me out of the line up to fight?" Braden asked.
"You are right. I'm not one that will bring down houses or crush humans – not on the outside anyway. But the mind, the mind is a completely different thing, and who better to test my skills on other than the greatest telepath in the world?" Hoyt says. He continues on, "There's a basketball court not too far from here. We should be able to have a peaceful match of minds there."

As they walk on the court, Braden says, "Are you sure you want to go through this young one?"

Hoyt laughs and says, "All you old guys feel like you are the strongest vampires around, but I'm here to prove you wrong."

As they stand in front of each other on the court, Hoyt holds his hand to his face and creates a V shape over his eye. A green hawk flies out of his eye and goes straight towards Braden who holds up his hand and tries to stop it with his telepathy. Hoyt busts out in laughter, "You can't stop something with your telepathy that isn't real old man."

The hawk flies into Braden's body and his neck snaps back and he sees his spirit come out of his body. When his spirit completely leaves his body, he can see his physical body just standing there like a blank canvas. In front of him, he sees Hoyt's spiritual presence as an all-white figure. They are instantly transferred into each other's body. As Braden looks down and sees Hoyt's hands and body, he looks up and says, "So this is your power, Hoyt?"

"Yes, my ability is called spiritual possession. I can take complete and total control of another person's body as you can already tell. I must admit your body feels good. I like being tall and your powers, I can feel coursing through me."

Hoyt continues on to say, "So this is what the most powerful mind feels like?"

Braden then says, "Like all old people, we are constantly disappointed in the youth of today. Here I thought you wanted to have a battle of the brains, yet you are nothing more than a thief and a disappointing battle."

"If I'm such a disappointment, I could just kill off the amazing body of yours and switch back at the last minute." Hoyt lifts the basketball pole out of the ground and slices it to where it now has a sharp edge. He looks at Braden and says, "Watch me impale you while you look on helplessly."

Hoyt sends the pole towards Braden's body and as he sees it coming, he raises both hands and waits for it to impale his body. As a couple of seconds pass, Hoyt pulls his head down and realizes that the pole is just sitting there in mid-air. He looks over at his old body and Braden is sitting in Indian style with the biggest smirk on his face.

Braden just starts to laugh and says, "You really are young and I can tell you are used to taking over peoples' bodies that are strong or have exceptional powers because you should know that taking over a person's body doesn't give you power over the mind. From the second we walked out the doors of the mansion I was reading your mind. I knew all about your plans to try and take over my body. I even know that you plan on turning on everyone and trying to kill

Norie soon. I've gone through all of your deep dark secrets and even when you took over my body, I read your mind on what you wanted to do and let you believe that was what you were doing by taking over my body. It was actually fun, but enough of the games, it's time to actually teach you a little something. In order to actually change spiritual places with a person and having plans to come back, there is always a hidden line that you travel back through. If I kill you, you may not make it back."

Hoyt is on the other side with a look of shock. He tries to move the pole from in front of him. Braden then says, "Don't panic young one, I don't plan to kill you just yet. I want to show you how helpless you are before I kill you." Braden moves the pole out of the way and throws it into the yard. He then looks back at Hoyt and says, "First thing I'm going to do is get my body back."

Hoyt laughs and says, "Only I can do that."

"Nah, I can make you get out of there. I could easily take over your mind and make you do it, but I think I will force your exit. How you might ask? Good question. Just let me know when you see them," Braden explains.

Hoyt then says, "How did ghouls get here?" Next thing you hear is Hoyt screaming in agony.

Braden says, "It feels so real, doesn't it? The ghouls eating away at your body. The mind is way more powerful than you think. Matter of fact, let's go back to when beheading was cool. I think I will run you through that a few times."

"Noooooooooo!!!!!!!" Hoyt yells in fear.

Braden laughs, "It's weird seeing your head leave your body, huh? Let's make sure you feel the burn."

In Hoyt's mind, his severed head sees a dragon come up and breathes flames all over his body. He begins to yell, "It's hot, it's hot, stop it please!!"

After seven minutes of torturous agony, eventually Hoyt leaves Braden's body in a panic and goes back to his own. Braden then looks down and sees his own hands and says, "My God Hoyt, you were terrified! My entire body is full of sweat. It's such a shame an old man like me put you in such a frenzy."

Hoyt is in such a broken state that he is shaking uncontrollably. He yells, "No one is afraid of you old man."

"We both know that is false, but I've given you enough playtime. To be truthful, your power is too different to leave you around. I couldn't picture you gaining control of one of the stronger members of Nomed's team."

Soon as he says that, Hoyt tries to leave his body again and Braden forces Hoyt's spirit back in his body with a wave of his hand. "Did you really think I would say that and actually let you do it? How naive do you think I am? I wish I could say this was entertaining but it was really nothing more than a consolation prize. I will destroy your mind before I kill you so you won't remember a thing."

Braden holds his hands towards Hoyt and Hoyt starts to feel his memories being stripped away from him. He begins to yell at Braden to give his thoughts back as he drops to his knees. As Braden was finished, Hoyt's body falls over, physically spent from what Braden has put him through. Braden walks over and sees Hoyt's eyes are glazed over and he is drooling out his mouth. Braden then says to himself, "It would be cruel of me to leave him here like this. I could at least kill him."

Braden looks over to the sharp pole from earlier, lifts it up with his powers and slams it through Hoyt's body. Braden then looks into the sky and says, "I haven't had this much fun in a long time. Maybe this was the right choice," as he begins to walk back to the house.

Mario & Maurice vs. Nomed & Turan

Nomed looks and says, "I really think I can take you and Maurice by myself to tell you the truth."

Maurice starts to laugh and says, "You might be right about having to fight us both, because I'm sure Turan won't last that long against me."

He looks at his brother and they both set their bodies a blaze. Mario has a red flame that surrounds his body and Maurice has a black flame around his body. In a flash Mario is in front of Nomed and he punches him into the stairwell with a vicious left hook. In reaction, Turan sets his body ablaze and a golden yellow flame emits from his body.

He notices Maurice sitting and looking at the fight with his brother so Turan runs up the other side of the stairwell and is throwing fireballs towards Maurice. As everything hits Maurice's black flame, they are absorbed. As Turan gets closer, he sets his entire back ablaze and tries to ram Maurice. As he does, Turan's entire flame is evaporated and Maurice grabs him by his neck and punches him in his stomach. Blood gushes out of his mouth and Maurice holds him over the balcony and drops him. Nomed gets to his feet and says, "So this is why they call you guys the dragon brothers. I'm actually pretty excited to fight you guys now. So one of you is fast and the other sends people's powers elsewhere?"

Mario says, "No stupid! My red flame that goes around my body is used to make me faster and make me stronger. The higher I turn the flame the faster and stronger I get. Maurice's black flame that surrounds his body is used to nullify other vampire's powers, so in other words, no matter what you throw at him he is able to cancel anything from hitting him."

"That is pretty much what I just said," Nomed said rolling his eyes. Nomed then yells at Turan and says, "Aren't you a master of flames? Why don't you know how to do this?"

Turan snaps at Nomed, "I've never seen this before, so how should I know how to create this? Nomed, you are really pissing me off." Turan then hurls a huge fireball toward Maurice and Maurice catches it head on. As he is absorbing it, Turan runs up the stairs and punches him off the balcony. As he looks down at Maurice's body he says, "You can't do both at the same time, huh?" Meanwhile, Mario sees this and tries to go attack Turan. He is caught in mid-air by Nomed and is kicked into the ground right beside his brother. Nomed reminds Mario, "Your battle is with me. You might need to focus on that."

Turan looks over at Nomed and says, "You know I had this under control, right? I didn't need you butting in."

"You are such a comedian. From what I was looking at you might not be able to win this one by yourself, so it's a good thing we are paired together."

Maurice jumps up and tries to hit Nomed. Nomed stops his punch and says, "You better ask Turan. Flames have no effect on me." In the same breath, Turan shoots a flame stream right towards Maurice, which he immediately absorbed and he once again focuses on Turan. By this time, Turan sees that he must switch in between flames and his normal strength.

"Let's see how long your stamina holds up during this fight because you are already winded," Maurice says.

Nomed finally looks back down at Mario, who is finally pulling himself out of the ground and spits blood. Nomed asks, "Are you ready to continue this battle or are you already done?"

Mario jumps up and attempts to hit Nomed in the face, but Nomed catches his fist with his hand and pulls him close and says, "Now you will see our difference in power," and he breaks his arm. Mario screams in pain and Maurice turns to see what has happened. In turn, Turan hits Maurice square in the chin with a punch. As he staggers back, he tells Turan, "I don't have time to waste with you anymore," and he creates the biggest black flame. He begins an onslaught of punches upon Turan's body. His powers are being used so much and trying to keep up with Turan that fatigue begins to set in.

Maurice continues to press in and he sweeps Turan to the ground. He begins to beat his face into the ground. Nomed smiles at the fact Mario is in pain and he kicks Mario's leg right where the joints meet and breaks it. He gives out another excruciating yell.

Once again, Maurice turns around and starts to walk away. As he does, Turan grabs his pants leg and stops him. Maurice turns around and kicks Turan's arm but it does not make him release it so Maurice bends down to punch him in the face. When he does this, Turan catches his fist while saying, "It took me a while to figure out a way to get my flames back but within doing so I've actually found a way to steal your powers. Now your flame is mine."

As Maurice's big black flame begins to dwindle down, Turan thanks him for the upgrade and then yells to Nomed, "I will leave the rest to you. It seems you were right, I did get my ass kicked," as he passes out.

Nomed cracks his neck and says, "Are you guys going to take turns or come at me together? I must admit I think coming at the same time will be more beneficial for you guys."

Mario and Maurice look at each other and shrug and say, "Why not? Let's get 'em ". Mario shares his red flame with Maurice and they speed towards Nomed. Nomed strengthens his stance and begins to block every punch that is thrown towards him. While laughing Nomed says, "This can't be the only power you have. If so, you picked the wrong one to leave standing."

Nomed jumps up and kicks Mario and twirls around and kicks Maurice with the other foot. As both of them go flying into the walls, Nomed looks at them struggling to get out.

"Are you sure you guys want to continue this?" Nomed asks them. Maurice says, "Don't you pity us! You will have to break us before we stop."

"Look at your brother. He is already broken up pretty bad and with him giving you some of his power he won't be able to heal as fast from broken bones, but if you want to be broken so be it," Nomed replied.

Maurice sees a red flash come near him and he blinks. When he opens his eyes, Nomed is right in front of him with a devilish grin on his face. Nomed then backhands Maurice and while his body is flying away, Nomed grabs his arm and the instant change in momentum dislocates it. Maurice screams in agony. Nomed then kicks him in his side and the bottom part of his body moves away from his top half and his body goes limp. Nomed looks at his body as it is now barely in one piece and says, "Remember you said you wanted this."

He then walks over to Mario, who is still inside the wall. The only thing you can see is his legs and arms dangling out of the hole he was kicked in. Nomed peeks inside the hole and sees a red pair of eyes. He starts to laugh and says, "Well, I see you're still alive in there Mario. I hope you don't think I've forgotten about our little plane ride to Atlantis a while ago. I told you we would handle our issue at another time, but I guess I'll give you a break since your brother so sincerely suggested it."

Right after saying that, Nomed grabs Mario's left leg and snaps it in two and then grabs his right and snaps that one in two as well. Mario screams so loud that even Markus hears him out in the yard. Nomed looks back into the black hole only to see one eye open and the other slowly going down. He says, "I'm sure you won't be moving anytime soon, but just in case, I'll break your right forearm as well." Mario doesn't even have enough power to show the pain he is in. He just grunts and passes out.

Afterwards Nomed goes and lays down on the part of Turan's body that's not in the ground. He grabs some gravel off of the ground and throws it in the hole where Turan's head is and says, "I guess we will chill here until everyone else finishes their battle."

"You know I can hear you, right? And stop being lazy and go fight Norie," Turan says.

"I'm not being lazy. I'm going to just sit here and listen to the battle. I just want to make sure no one gets killed so if I'm needed I'm not held up fighting Norie. Plus, most of the battles have already ended already."

Turan asks, "How do you know that?"

Nomed says, "That's because Arnoldo and Braden are in the room looking at your inglorious self. You would be able to see them if you could lift your head."

"Just shut the fuck up and let me know when everyone comes back okay."

Kali vs. Shelby

Shelby's eyes open and she realizes that she is flying through the air and she thinks to herself, *"How the hell did this happen?"* As she looks down she says, "I guess I might as well prepare for myself to ground." As Shelby approaches the ground, she braces herself and her body hits and skids across the ground.

"That wasn't as bad as I thought it would be," she thought to herself.

As she looks up, Kali is in front of her and says, "I thought you would have blocked that, but I see you can't see things that are invisible. This should be an easy fight for me."

Kali once again turns invisible and Shelby hears a loud clonk sound as if a bird ran into a window. Shelby starts to laugh, "So how did running into my invisible force field feel?"

Kali reappears with a bruise on her forehead, "So, I can become invisible and you can make invisible force fields. It seems like I picked the wrong person to battle against. How about we say forget the invisible stuff and do this hand to hand so we don't have to fight all night until the sun comes up and we both die."

"I wouldn't die. If that was only the case, then my power is more in depth than that, but if you want to have a true fist fight, then I'm down for that," Shelby says.

Kali starts to jump up and down stretching and says, "I haven't been able to have a good dog fight with a chick in a long time. Don't be mad when I smash in that pretty face."

"Enough talk, let's do this." She runs towards Kali and swings with a right hook. At the same time, Kali swings with a right hook of her own. They both connect at the same time and they send each other flying to the ground. Kali rushes up and runs towards Shelby, who is still on the ground.

As she bends down to punch her, Shelby kicks her in the stomach and Kali staggers back. As Shelby gets to her feet, she is punched back to her knees by Kali, who is then swept off her feet by Shelby. As Kali falls towards the ground, they both catch each other's eyes and exchange blows once again. Both struggle to get up, but as Shelby finally gets to her feet she looks over at Kali and says, "I see your lip is bleeding."

"You might want to look in the mirror because so is yours. It seems like it was probably in our best interest to pick each other because it seems you don't fight much either. I figured you hanging around with Nomed, you would at least be a better fighter."

Shelby's face turns stern and says, "You wouldn't make it five more minutes against me."

Kali replies with a smirk, "Now that is the person I'm looking for." Shelby charges at Kali and is immediately kicked in her side. Shelby begins to lift off her feet but catches Kali's leg to hold her ground and brings back the momentum from her kick and hits Kali square in the nose with her elbow. The blood starts to flow from Kali's nose and she wipes the blood from her nose. She turns her arms and feet invisible and runs towards Shelby, who yells, "You have no honor. We agreed not to use powers, you coward!"

Kali begins to hit Shelby with kicks and fists, one after the other. Shelby tries to time the movements as she sees her body sway from side to side, but between the darkness and her eyes not being able to see, she doesn't see the blows coming towards her. As Shelby gets turned around and around, she finally puts up her shield and Kali's movements are stopped as her fist slams and breaks against her shield.

Shelby begins to laugh and says, "You know what? I've begun to notice that since I've drank human blood that my shield has gotten stronger. I am able to walk in the sun longer, and I can make my shield into a weapon."

Kali says, "A weapon, huh? If that was the case, you would have shown me that earlier."

"Truth be told, I just wanted to see how strong you really were and now that I know you are weak and of no honor I now have no problem showing you my true power," Shelby says.

Shelby holds up her right hand and brings it down towards Kali's right arm. Kali screams in pain. Her right arm becomes visible as it is laying on the ground. Shelby walks over and picks up her arms and begins to suck the blood out of it.

She looks at Kali and says, "The real reason I wanted the fight between us to last longer is to see if your blood would be worth drinking and it is soooo sweet."

Kali runs towards her and says, "There is no way I would let you mock me by drinking my blood."

Before she reaches Shelby, she is kicked into an invisible chair. Kali yells, "I can't move! What have you done, you bitch?"

Shelby replies, "I have bound you to an invisible chair with restraints. You won't be able to go anywhere. I am going to take my time drinking your blood until it's all gone."

Kali says, "You have become blood thirsty. Only a few vampires that can't control their thirst actually enjoy feeding on vampires. The others who just have a thirst only seek out humans. What you are, there is no cure for. Even if you kill me here, eventually your friends will have to kill you in order to save you. You might have won this battle but I will eventually win the war."

Shelby walks up to her and says, "I can endure whatever comes my way and Nomed will never let me be killed. No one will find out anytime soon because you will be dead," and Shelby begins to drink her blood from the place where she cut her arm. She even takes the time to create a suction device and an invisible cup. Kali begins to yell for help as loud as she can. Shelby looks and says, "You can yell all you want, but no one is around us and no one will save you at this moment."

Shelby has the most demonic look on her face. Shelby holds her head down and looks Kali in the eyes and says, "Maybe I should slit your neck. I might get more blood from there and you will shut up."

Kali says, "I surrender! You have won."

"Now you have honor, now you have a code? It matters not! You will die here," Shelby says.

Shelby holds back her hand and swings it towards Kali's neck. As it comes down towards Kali's neck, her arm suddenly is stopped.

A big figure illuminates behind her. As she turns and looks to see who is behind her, Arnoldo is standing with her arm in his hand.
"I haven't felt a thirst for blood as deep as yours in years and from what I just witnessed, you need help."
"Let me go before I kill you," Shelby yells.
"As if someone as weak as you could kill me," Arnoldo says.

Shelby then turns her blade towards him and sends her left arm crashing towards his body. You can hear the blade break against his chest.

Arnoldo looks and says, "I knew this would be your answer. We will work on your blood thirst after this mission. If I wasn't familiar with the feeling of thirsty vampires I wouldn't have ever sensed this and you would have spiraled down a road you could never come back from." Arnoldo then knocks Shelby unconscious immediately.
Kali says, "Yes, thank you for saving me."
Arnoldo says, "I didn't care what happened to you. I only came here to save Shelby from herself."

Kali turns invisible and tries to run away to safety. Arnoldo put Shelby in his arm and starts to run. He grabs at the air and grabs thin air and holds it up above him.
"Unlike untrained vampires, you can turn invisible, but you can't stop yourself from breathing. I can hear that as if you were visible."

After a few more seconds pass, Kali's body becomes visible and her hands are frantically trying to free her neck from Arnoldo's grip. It is of no use and within fifteen more seconds she is unconscious as well. Arnoldo puts her under his other arm and turns around and walks towards the mansion.

Markus vs. Gillie

Gillie looks down towards his hands and says, "I am glad that I put my hands up to block that or it would have hurt a little."
Gillie glides through the sky and does a backflip and lands gently to the ground. He notices that he landed not too far from the house and Markus is walking towards him dragging his scythe. It's cutting through anything it touches with ease. Gillie says to himself, *"I can't get touched by that or it's over for me."*

Markus walks towards Gillie and ask, "Why have you guys decided to go against the system and why would you guys want to challenge Norie?"

Gillie replies, "It's simple – we are tired of being slaves and living in a system. We want to be free and make our own decisions. We aren't trying to take over the world, we just want to live in peace."

Markus begins to laugh and says, "You really think the humans will let you guys just run amuck on something they have worked so hard to gain?"

Gillie interrupts, "You meant to say something they stole? This world has been ours since the beginning of time. They are merely adopting it for a little while, but enough about me, my question is why are you serving Norie and what do you owe to him?"

"I owe him nothing. My brothers and I just decided we would rather be in a position of power than with the bottom feeders."

"You guys are the reason most vampires aspire to work under someone than to go out and get their own positions of power."

Markus says, "Do you guys know that anyone who openly challenges the kings have never been heard of since their battles? They have all been defeated and killed! How many people are trying to go down that road?"

"At least they died with honor and dignity instead of being stuck serving under someone they thought they were stronger than, so let's get this battle started so we can show you guys how to take down a king."

Markus then says cockily, "This battle won't be long. We know all of your abilities and powers. For example, Gillie you can move through time for short amounts and can shoot black bolts through those oddly shaped guns of yours. But this here scythe of mine gives me the ability to actually *see* where and when you move through time."

Markus then rushes towards Gillie with his scythe and swings it towards Gillie, who dodges it before going forward in time. Markus immediately makes his scythe the size of a small sword and plunges it into Gillie's arm.

Gillie smirks at him, and Markus says, "What are you smiling at?"

Gillie replies, "I didn't think you were telling the truth about being able to follow me. I guess I'll let you in on a little secret. Since drinking human blood, my powers have matured."
Markus says, "How does that matter to me? As long as I have this scythe you couldn't possibly beat me."

Markus charges at Gillie again and swings his sword. Gillie pulls his gun and shoots a bolt towards Markus' scythe and it is knocked away. As Markus closes in on Gillie, he smiles and from his gun he fires a bolt that only comes out halfway. It creates a sword from the barrel of his gun and clashes with Markus' scythe. The sword Gillie created pulls him forward, minimizes his sword and stabs it directly into Markus' shoulder. Markus has a look of amazement on his face.

Gillie looks and says, "Oh, you thought only you could do that, huh? Well let me show you what else I can do, Markus." Gillie teleports in front of Markus and at that exact moment, Markus hears his brother Mario scream in agony and pain. In that split second, the match between he and Gillie no longer matters. He turns and starts to run towards the house. Gillie time shifts in front of him and kicks him back to where they were originally fighting. Markus, in a rage, increases the size of his scythe and says, "Either you can move out of my way or I will move you. This is no longer a game."
Gillie says, "This was never a game, so come at me with all you've got."

Markus speeds towards him and swings the massive scythe towards Gillie who does not move out of the way. In Gillie's hand is a hand full of the dark matter from Markus' scythe. Markus pulls back the pole of his scythe in confusion.

Gillie then says, "I told you I was different. From the moment you pierced my body with that scythe I realized it's the matter I've been using to power my guns and I've used and been around this matter for far longer than you even. If you had lived from the beginning when the world was created, I would still have worked with this matter longer than you. When I move through time it's as if time does not exist I could literally be gone for 20 minutes and in the other realm years have passed. I wish I could just wait for things to happen or interrupt them. To make a long story short, you couldn't possibly harm me with that thing, no matter how hard you tried. Why do you think you can find me when I time shift but only when the scythe is in your hands?"

Markus interrupts him immediately, "Who says I was wrong to doubt your powers? I am not ashamed to admit that. I have been completely out classed. I will not try to stop what you guys are doing. Now, I just want to go make sure my brothers are still alive."
"Since you said it so nicely, I have no problem letting you go check on them. Too bad your brothers are in trouble. This has been a fun duel. But to be honest, your brothers chose the wrong person to fight. Nomed is the strongest physically between all of us. The only person I think that could go toe to toe with him is Braden. Speaking of, let's hurry back to the mansion to make sure they are even still alive."

Narkisa vs. Leo

Leo blocks Narkisa's initial swing with his blade. It makes a loud shrieking noise, as if her nails were made out of blades. In the midst of being amazed by Narkisa's powers, he was kicked into the next room, a large library. As he went crashing through the large table, Leo plants his swords firmly in the ground to keep him from continuing to move backwards. As he looks up, Narkisa is walking through the broken door licking her fingers saying, "Your swords sure are sharp. They might have nicked my fingers. If you haven't noticed by now, my fingers are as hard as steel. Your swords won't be able to work that well against me."

"You must not know who I am? I am the number one swordsman in the world. There's no steel that I can't cut."

"We shall put that theory to the test tonight," Narkisa says as she rushes at him moving from side to side.

Leo pulls his swords out of the ground as he rushes towards her as well. As they clash, Leo begins to twirl and dance around his blades as if they were an extension of his hands. Amazingly enough, Narkisa is evading every blade with the greatest of ease. Finally, Narkisa strikes back in mid-air, dodging as she scratches Leo's shoulder.

Immediately Leo jumps back and says, "I did notice my blades had a purple liquid on them. So that is your secret? Your nails are filled with toxin and from the feeling of it entering my body it seems to have a numbing effect."

Leo goes inside his cloak and pulls out a small knife and stabs it into his shoulder. He moves it around ever so gently and he pulls the blade out and on the tip is the purple toxin that was injected into his body. He looks at Narkisa and says, "If this is the way you plan to win against me it won't ever work. My body can recognize any foreign thing that enters my body. I've trained my body to not allow it to enter my bloodstream so it is easier to retrieve from my body so I am not compromised." He drops the toxin on the floor, "Let me ask you this, Narkisa, do you know everything on earth moves at its own sound frequency? What makes me the best swordsman in the world is that I have the ability to hear them all."

Leo gets in a stance and says, *"dark flower rising"* and instantly he is behind Narkisa. He hits her in the sky with his swords and jumps above her and pulls out his katana and puts them all together. He tells Narkisa, "Now you will witness eternal darkness," and he plunges the swords into her stomach. As they fall into the ground, he notices that the blades did not penetrate. Leo feels two blades in his back. He looks at her hands and notices they are nowhere near him. He adjusts himself and realizes she has cut him using her toes.

As he pulls out a blade to remove the poison, Narkisa nonchalantly gets up and says, "I forgot to tell you, I can use my feet as a weapon as well. Let me get these shoes off of my babies." She kicks each shoe off her foot. "Also, I forgot to tell you I trained my body to be extremely strong against weapons. I wonder how much longer you are going to be able to get my toxin out of your body now."

Leo drops the blades with the toxins on them to the ground and says, "I will never run out of swords, but now I will show you one of my favorite swords and one of my more deadly ones." He pulls a yellow sword from behind his back. Leo goes on, "I usually only use dull swords to fight because the real sharp ones tend to end my battles faster. This one has no dull side to it, so this should be quick." He crouches down and says, *"autumn seahorse,"* and goes directly towards Narkisa, slicing her stomach. The blood starts to flow from her body.

Narkisa says, "So you have been holding out your true power, Leo? I feel a little jaded."

"If I would have taken this seriously from the beginning, the battle would have been over already."

Leo holds his sword towards the ground and says, *"hell raiser."* As he slashes the ground, the boards from the floor begin to raise up and his slash goes right across Narkisa's chest. The blow makes her twirl in the air before hitting the ground. Narkisa is slow to get up as she staggers to her feet. She looks at Leo and says, "I guess you leave me no choice." She then starts to excrete a huge amount of toxin from her fingertips and she jams her fingers into her body. Leo's eyes grow big as he witnesses Narkisa transform into the serpent like creature. Her skin is now green and purple, with dots and scales everywhere.

Narkisa looks up and says, "Few have seen this form of mine. I'm sure you don't even know what kind of beast is in front of you. Norie told me that it was once a race of vampires that had successfully fused with the Gizmodo lizard, the most dangerous predator in the world. They have razor sharp claws and no natural predators due to its toxins. I am the one that carries our culture to the world and with that being said, it is now time that I destroy you."

She begins to move from side to side again but this time it's to the point Leo can barely follow her movements. Narkisa attacks Leo's legs as he narrowly blocks it with his sword. By the time his eyes catch her again, she has scratched his entire back. The marks are so big that Leo can't remove the toxin with a sword, he just stands there not moving with his eyes closed.

Narkisa says, "My toxins are more powerful in this form. It seems as if they are moving extremely fast throughout your body now, so you won't be able to move shortly."

Leo lets out a loud roar that continues to go on for a minute, he looks up and said, "Remember that I have trained my body, Narkisa. I just had to take some time to push it out of my body using just my muscles." Leo lets out one more roar and a purple cloud sprays out of his back, with sweat dripping from his forehead.

"It took longer than expected, but now I see that I can no longer play any games. I will let you meet Shesharuu, the serpent dragon. Leo unsheathes the blue blade from behind his back. As it is coming out of its sheath, it has this light blue glow to it and Leo's body seems to be being pushed back from the force of the sword. He adjusts his grip and says, "This dragon always tries to tell me who is in charge."

Narkisa says, "There really is a powerful dragon locked in there. I can feel it. How do you even have something so powerful under your control?"

Leo says, "This sword was given to me after my greatest defeat as a constant reminder that I would never be strong enough even with this wonderful sword to defeat that man."

Leo tightens his grip, looks at Shesharuu and says, "Take two of her fingers." He swings his sword towards Narkisa and all she feels is a gust of wind and two of her fingers are flying up in the sky.

She immediately panics and says, "How the fuck did you do that?! I wasn't even touched by anything!"

Leo says, "I told you game time is over, didn't I? Whatever I tell Shesharuu to attack that's just what he does, and if you're not fast enough to see him you will never stop the attack. Now it's time to end this game," and he looks down at Shesharuu once again and tells him to take out the bottom part of her spine.

Upon hearing this, Narkisa begins to evade the gust of wind that is coming her way. As Narkisa is running throughout the library room, she turns around and she can see this big long blue dragon chasing her.

Leo says, "So even in your frantic state, you're actually moving fast enough to see him, huh? He is a marvelous creature isn't he? Unfortunately though, that won't help you, even in this battle. Shesharuu! End this now!" Upon that request, the dragon creates two paths of wind on both sides of Narkisa.

As she turns around, she realizes there are actually wings blocking her way and then Shesharuu's head flies toward her. Sheharuu enters her stomach and comes out of her back and Narkisa hits the ground. Leo sheathes his sword and says, "Now you know why I am feared around the world, and don't worry, your body parts won't grow back for a while. At least not until he completely digests them then they will be back in the physical world. That usually takes two weeks, so sit tight and I'll be back to get you shortly."

Narkisa lays on the ground paralyzed and says, "Fuck you, Leo. You cheated."

Leo replies, "There is no such thing as cheating in battle," and he walks off back into the other room.

Wynn vs. Calderon

Calderon was blown out of the mansion and falls into a tree. The entire time, Calderon was caught inside a wind vortex that Wynn created. At first, he found himself just riding its rhythm as if he was surfing and only fell out and hit the tree when he concentrated to see who was blown out the house after him. He started laughing when he saw it was Demetri. "He looks like a crash dummy floating through the air," Calderon thought as he watched him get pulverized out of the house. As he gathers himself out the tree, Wynn walks up to him and says, "So, I heard you were a master of the elements, Calderon. I didn't think something that small would send you flying off like that."

Calderon starts to laugh and says, "Very funny, pops. You really think something that lame could really do any damage to me?" "What's lame is that I don't understand you younger generation of vampires and your way of talking," Wynn says rolling his eyes. "Well let me put you up on game, gramps. Lame is the equivalent to boring or weak, in which your initial attack was both. I had to take on your little gust of wind as a joy ride."

Wynn gets infuriated and sends two wind blades towards Calderon. As it slices through the ground in front of him, Calderon just holds up both hands and catches them. As they shake and rattle in his hand he looks at Wynn and says, "These things are dangerous. You could really hurt someone with these," as he grips the wind blades and destroys them in his hand.

Wynn says, "You are such an insolent and disrespectful vampire." You can hear the frustration in his voice.

Calderon interrupts and says, "You have to earn my respect and so far your power won't gain that prize."

Wynn then creates a massive wind and sends it towards Calderon, who creates a house made of water and just sits there in a water made chair, looking and laughing at Wynn.

Calderon creates a small window and says, "Did you forget I'm an elemental? I just made my water spin in the opposite direction and let all that nasty wind pass through."

Wynn then sends four massive blades of wind towards the house. As they come winding towards him, Calderon manipulates the water to where it bends the blades away from the house and they keep flowing through the yard.

Calderon says, "This is really not working in your favor, pops." "Don't you patronize me," Wynn says through clenched teeth at Calderon.

Calderon continues to watch Wynn begin to prepare to create a tornado to attempt to destroy him and his house. As he is creating a massive tornado, Calderon builds an earth cell right on top of him and sits on the ground waiting to see what happens. He sits and watches the clay house move up and down as he sees that Wynn is trying to force himself out of the house. Five minutes go by and finally Calderon starts to see the clay house start to crack and finally the house burst into pieces and the wind throws the pieces everywhere. Wynn has broken out into a sweat and gets madder as he sees how amused Calderon is at the fact he was stuck in that house. Calderon says, "You should really not be that mad, old timer. I really could have made that house out of a harder material and way more layers or even closed it at the bottom. I thought I was really doing you a favor."

Wynn, now fed up with Calderon's antics and smug attitude, creates a cyclone the size of a mountain. Calderon flicks a gust of wind right in the middle of the cyclone and it completely negates it. Wynn sits and looks confused and slightly amazed and says, "How can you possibly make something so big disappear in seconds?"

Calderon says, "You old guys always believe that making things bigger is the key to showing your power, but truth is size really doesn't matter. All I did was create a small wind ball going in the opposite direction that your cyclone was and made sure that it was ten times *stronger* than your cyclone. Matter of fact, let me teach you a little something." Calderon flicks a mini tornado the size of his hand towards Wynn. As it hits his body, his face goes from being calm to utter pain.

The tornado feels like a million punches to his stomach. Wynn begins coughing up blood and drops to his knees.

Calderon walks over to Wynn and says, "See gramps? The smaller ones are more compact and they can do more damage because they are so much more powerful in condensed sizes."

Wynn yells, "I won't be mocked by someone like you," and he creates four hurricanes and sends them towards Calderon. Calderon nonchalantly shrugs and walks right towards them, stretches out his arms and grabs two of them and busts them apart. For the next one, he throws one of his elemental balls at it and completely freezes it. For the last hurricane, he walks up and grabs it by the bottom and lets it dance over his head and over seconds it gets smaller and smaller until it turns to dust in his hand.

Calderon looks and says, "Wynn, we are on two completely different levels. You couldn't possibly dream of beating me. Let me show you how far the younger generation has passed you." Calderon then grabs both Wynn's feet by moving the earth beneath his feet and turning them into shackles around Wynn. Wynn tried to tear them off using his wind powers, but Calderon creates water cyclone gloves over his hands that stop him from using his powers. Wynn frantically tries to blow the water off his hands but it's pointless. The rotation of the water is so strong, the wind won't even form.

Calderon then throws air punches towards him. They are hitting his body so hard that the imprints from the last punch can be seen coming out of his back. Calderon walks up to the now completely bloody Wynn and says, "Have you had enough old man?" and Wynn spits blood in his face.

Calderon gets mad and says, "You disrespectful old fuck," and Calderon turns his hand into a giant boulder and uses his powers over wind to create a rocket booster for his punch and he uppercuts Wynn out of the shackles that were holding him into the ground. Wynn's body flies up in the sky and his eyes turn white as his lifeless body hits the ground.

Calderon says to himself, "Oh shit. Nomed did say give them the option to join us and not just kill them." He then reaches for an elemental ball of electricity and he crushes it in his hand. With the electrical bolt in his hand he rams it into Wynn's body. Wynn's body lifts up in a 'V' shape and he makes a big gasp for air.

Calderon stands in front of him with an electric sword and says, "Now that you're alive – make a choice, live or die again. You live, as long as you promise not to interfere with us and protect this house; or I can kill you again and you can go to whatever place I just sent you. Which one is it, pops?"

Wynn quickly replies and says, "I will follow you guys, I will follow!"

Calderon then reaches down his hand to help Wynn up. As soon as Wynn reaches to grab his hand, Calderon moves it and Wynn falls back. Calderon says, "I still haven't forgotten you spit in my face. Help yourself up or lay there old timer," and he walks off.

Wynn lays there watching him walk off and thinks to himself, "The youth really have blossomed into some amazing vampires. Their power can even rival the Gods," and he passes out.

Dunkan vs. Demetri

As Demetri is hit by the sound waves, he thinks to himself, *"Hmmm, should I stop my body or just keep floating?"* He looks around and says to himself, *"Ahhhhh I'll just keep floating, it's peaceful."* He passes by Braden and says, "Fancy meeting you here!" and Braden just looks at him like he is crazy. Demetri is wondering how much longer will I keep floating back. He passes a few birds and fireflies as he continues to float through the sky.

As he looks back towards the way he came, he sees Dunkan following him. He yells, "You are a fast little shit. I think my body is going at least 30 mph and you're keeping up."

His body continues to float through the air and eventually he crashes into a fountain in front of the estate. Demetri gets up and cracks his neck and says, "Man I thought that ride was never going to end." He faces Dunkan and says, "So let me return the favor you just gave me."

Demetri rushes Dunkan and is sent back into the fountain by Dunkan with just the snap of his fingers.
Dunkan says, "You must think that I can only yell. A lot of people have this misconception. I can create sound waves using any part of my body mentally: it's called Sonokinesis. Also, I've done my research on you Demetri. You are known as a crazed fighter, one who loses his cool, and tends to get lost in his fights. Someone like you couldn't possibly dream of defeating me. I actually could take my time and plan out my attacks against you. When it comes to you I just have to keep you away from me and fight like a tactician."

Demetri laughs and says, "Do you really think you can run from me? If you want to play a game of cat and mouse I'm down for the challenge." Once again, he charges Dunkan and when he swings, Dunkan glides away from him and ends up right beside him, and with a sound wave powered punch he sends Demetri to the ground.
"See? You rushed in once again not fully grasping my powers. All I did was use my sound powers to move away from your punch and end up beside you. I can use the sound in the air to freely increase my speed and agility," Dunkan said.

Demetri gets up and says, "You little shit! You really think a punk with fans for hands could possibly defeat me?!" and rushes towards Dunkan again and started throwing an array of punches that Dunkan floats around with the biggest smile on his face.
Demetri says, "What the fuck are you smiling at? Don't mock me! Once I catch you and beat up that pretty little face of yours, you won't be smiling after that."

While the battle is going on, Demetri notices that Dunkan put his hand to his mouth and then takes it away, Demetri says, "Do you plan on throwing spit on me or did you just throw up a little bit in fear of me?"

Dunkan says, "I'm smiling because I have nothing to fear from you. What's in my hand you will just have to see to believe" as he keeps his hand closed while moving in towards Demetri.

Dunkan says, "Do you really think your fist can keep me away from you? Let's be serious. Your caliber of fighting is no match for me," as he closes in and gets face to face with Demetri. He opens his hand by Demetri's stomach. Demetri is sent flying into a tree, with blood gushing out of his mouth upon impact.

The tree falls over as Demetri pulls himself out of the bark. At this point, all Demetri can see is red. He picks up both halves of the trees and throw them at Dunkan who easily moves and knocks them out of the way by merely moving his hands.

Dunkan says, "Do you really think that you throwing things is going to get you somewhere with me if your fist can't even touch me?"

Demetri punches the ground in frustration and watches it crumble under Dunkan. He moves out of the way and in an instant Demetri is right beside him and throws a massive punch. Dunkan guards himself with a sound shield but even the shield can't stand the destructive force behind the punch and Dunkan is hurled into the broken fountain.

Dunkan gathers himself and says, "So I see that your rage is not your weakness, it is your strength. You not only get powerful while you are in this state but your senses are heightened also. You have gone mute and are only focused on the fight. You're no longer your normal talkative self. So this is what it's like to look death in the face during a battle?"

Demetri says nothing, he just charges in towards Dunkan. Dunkan says, "So you are going to try the same method once again," and as Demetri swings Dunkan avoids, but this time Demetri follows his movements and is in the same place Dunkan was trying to escape to.

Dunkan swings with a sonic punch and Demetri dodges but flows along with the punch. The ones that follow Demetri dodges with ease and kicks Dunkan in his side, who in turns hits him with another sonic blast. Dunkan goes rolling through the ground and as he catches Demetri, he notices that Demetri was barely phased by the sonic blast. Demetri then rushes him again and Dunkan sends sound waves to try to stop him. Demetri jumps, dodges, and spins past them.

As he reaches Dunkan, he goes in his pocket and pulls out a flask and drink everything inside of it. Demetri begins to stumble and rocks back and forth, but then leaps forward and smashes Dunkan in the face with a punch that sends him flying.

Dunkan keeps himself from being thrown too far by the punch. He yells to Demetri, "That was some cowardly move, Demetri! And here I was thinking to myself I didn't want to fight a drunk, but truth be told I see I can no longer take you as a joke. I don't even know why I'm speaking to you it's not like you can hear me anymore anyway."

Dunkan rushes Demetri this time who is staggering back and forth, and as he reaches him, Demetri stands completely still and he changes his fighting style to Krav Maga and begins to target Dunkan's most vital points and vulnerable parts on his body. Dunkan goes on the defense and as he does, Demetri turns his stance to Muay Thai and leaps, elbowing Dunkan in his head. Once again, Dunkan is sent flying back, thinking to himself, *"So this is the infamous Demetri I've heard so much about being able to switch through so many styles at the drop of a hat, along with not being concerned with anything but his enemies. If only he could be this proficient without losing his mind, I would be in extreme trouble with fighting him."*

In no time, Demetri is flipping in front of him once again, switching his style to ninjutsu and moving as gracefully as a feather floating down to the ground. Dunkan then realizes he must finish this now before Demetri switches styles to something deadlier or more forbidden than the style before it.

As Demetri is flipping, he is caught by sound shackles as he struggles to be free of the binding sounds. Dunkan jumps above him and yells sound waves down upon him drilling him into the ground. As the waves keep coming, Demetri goes further into the ground. His ears begin to bleed and upon noticing, Dunkan gets closer and starts to yell directly into his face and says, "I will end this now. You put up a great fight Demetri, but it's time to die."

Once he is right in front of Demetri's face, Demetri's eyes go from being glazed over in a crazed rage back to the normal emerald green they are and Dunkan feels his throat suddenly closing. He looks down and notices Demetri has grabbed him by his neck and is crushing it. As he looks into Demetri's eyes, Demetri says, "It's been a while since someone has been able to knock me out of a crazed rage, but thanks to that I figured out the only way to get you close enough for me to hurt you is that I had to make you believe that you had me on the finish line. But soon as I realized you were close enough for me to touch, and you were so focused on my pain you let go of your shackles, so it is only right that I take advantage of that."

Dunkan frantically starts to hit Demetri with sound attacks, but it's to no avail. He has to stop in order to try to get Demetri to loosen his grip, but it doesn't work. As the seconds pass, eventually his throat is crushed and he passes out. Demetri slowly gets up, throws Dunkan over his shoulder and begins to walk towards the mansion. His ears are still blown so all he hears are the sirens going off in his ears.

As he reaches the house, he drops Dunkan. Then he yells to Nomed, "I didn't get a chance to ask him who's side he was on, so I left him alive." Right after making that statement, he passes out in front of everyone and his body crashes to the ground. As everyone walks over to check on him, they realize he had the biggest smirk on his face.

Gillie says, "Look Nomed, he took a tip out of your book and crushed his throat. Remember you did that to Dr. Kegal?"

Calderon looks on and says, "I remember that," and laughs.

Arnoldo says, "Demetri barely won the fight and passed out, but I'm sure he is dreaming happily about fighting, you can tell."

Norie vs. Nomed

Nomed walks over and says, "I really expected him to be in condition to move on after his fight, so with him being passed out, Shelby being knocked out, and Turan debating getting up I think it's time for us to go visit Norie. Can you guys help carry our wounded? Markus, do you plan on showing us the way or even coming at all, or are you going to sit here and see how things pan out?"

Markus looks at Nomed and says, "I'm going to stay here and tend to my brothers. I have no interest in watching this battle. I'll at least tell you how to get to him. Once you go up the stairs, just walk straight back and you will reach this giant door with a picture of a battle with the werewolves on it. On the other side, you will find Norie."

Nomed says, "Thank you Markus, I'll see you in a little while. Try not to go that far."

"You guys are one cocky lot of people," Markus says as Nomed and his team walk off.

The rest of the team follows him up the stairs. Arnoldo is carrying Demetri and Shelby, and Turan is finally up and back to his normal self.

As they walk down the hall, he is asking everyone, "Why do old people tend to collect all this old shit in their houses?" He turns and looks at a set of old battle armor and says, "Check this out. What the hell do you need this in the hallway for? Let's just look around. It looks like we are walking into the past. I don't think anything here is from the last five hundred years! It has to been two thousand years or more."

As they approach Norie's door, they see this amazing and gigantic silver door with figures made out of diamonds, rubies, and jewels. Nomed approaches it and says, "You have to respect this battle. Whoever did this door really captured the moment."

As he pushes open the door, he finds Norie sitting on a throne with a cup of blood in his hand. Norie looks up and says, "I wasn't expecting this many of you guys to actually make it here. I guess I underestimated you guys. Oh well, it matters not. I will just have to do things myself and take you all out."

He gets out of his seat and raises both of his hands. Leo, Turan, and Shelby's bodies begin to rise into the air.

Turan yells, "What the fuck is going on?"

Braden jumps in and says, "Look at your wounds! He is drawing the blood out of them."

As he finishes his statement their bodies move rapidly towards Norie, who in turn releases some of the blood in his capsule and creates a human sized bat. As they reach him, he slugs all three bodies into the wall.

Norie then creates three javelin like blades and tosses them towards Leo, Turan, and Shelby. Arnoldo, Gillie, and Nomed rush in. Gillie slows one of the javelins down and shoots it down with his gun. Arnoldo grabs one and breaks it in half, and Nomed kicks the last one up into the ceiling. Nomed then looks at Norie and says,

"How about we keep this fight between us? I didn't even know an old geezer like you even knew how to use a baseball bat."

"Who do you think gave humans the idea to create the sport? You don't even know your people's history. Do you really believe that you are worthy of being a vampire king without knowing simple history?" Norie laughs.

Nomed says, "Worthy? My father was the original king of all vampires. You were even under him."

Norie interrupts and says, "You are nothing more than a lab rat and your father isn't here, so nobody cares about his previous achievements!"

"You are a coward, Norie! You didn't even try to save my father. You just wanted his seat here. There are rats more noble than you are. How can you even call yourself his pupil when you gave up on your maker and let the humans take over and use him as a lab experiment? That is the main reason I am going to take you all down one by one and become the one and only vampire king and then I will find my father and I will free him during the process. I will eliminate all of the people who let our kind suffer at the hands of humans."

"You little ingrate! Do you think we haven't tried to find out where he was or even break free from the hold on the humans? They have every vampire's blood. There's no way we could have beat them."

Nomed says, "You not only are you a coward but you're also a liar."

He pulls out a necklace with a golden amulet on it he says, "You know what this is right? Let's see if it works." He says, *"alon tatarus demon,"* and nothing happens to any vampire in the room.

Nomed then says, "So are you telling me that they had your blood? That doesn't mean shit! You so called 'kings' sat by and did nothing in order to return a favor from the noble houses.

Norie begins to laugh and says to Nomed, "You believe you have it all figured out, don't you Nomed? I agreed to some terms in order to be set free and there are some things we do in this world where you have to see the bigger picture and this was one of those times, but I don't owe you an explanation to anything I do at any time you ungrateful lab rat! Since you are in the business of calling people rats, or how did you put it, I'm lower than rats, so that would mean that you are above me right?"

Nomed replies, "I was better than you the moment I was created. Now enough of this chit chat. Let's get this battle over with. I've been waiting to crack your face in since that plane trip we took together to Atlantis."

"Well there is no better chance than right now for you to try to accomplish that goal young child."

"I am nobody's child," Nomed says as he cracks his knuckles and walks towards Norie.

Nomed wastes no time as he rushes Norie and throws a punch, but immediately, Norie creates a giant shield and it stops Nomed's punch. The shield grabs his hand and then a hole opens up and Norie delivers a gut-wrenching kick to Nomed's side that sends him flying.

As Nomed's body skids across the floor he catches himself and says, "So that is all that you've got, huh?"

Nories laughs and says, "I had to make sure you can handle basic kicks without becoming a cripple."

Norie then holds out his hands and blood floats in the air out of his capsule and it goes into his hand. He creates a pair of kamas and begins to twirl them in his hands and dashes towards Nomed. As he swings the kamas at Nomed, they are easily evaded.

Nomed smirks and says, "If this is your plan you need to go back to the drawing board."

Norie continues to slash at Nomed who continues to easily move around the blades. Norie then tightens his grip while swinging and enlarges his kamas to giant scythes. In doing so, he cuts Nomed from his chest to his stomach. Nomed then leaps back at a faster speed until he is out of the range of Norie's giant scythes. He thinks to himself, *"Good thing I wasn't using my full speed, 'cause if he had that timed out I would have been in big trouble."*

Norie yells, "For someone so confident, you ran far away from my scythes. Your problem, and probably your downfall is that you are too cocky and you don't assess your enemies powers because you think that you can just over power them."

"You are the person against the ropes here. That cheap parlor trick won't work on me again."

"You think extending my weapons is the extent of my power? You must be crazy. I haven't even begun to show you what I'm capable of."

Nomed says, "Well how about you fight like a man?"

Norie interrupts and says, "I owe no type of loyalty to you, nor do I respect you but to decline a challenge from a mere vampire would tarnish my name."

Norie then holds his hands up again and they are covered in blood. The blood hardens and creates gloves protecting his hands. Then in an instant, he is front of Nomed and lands a blow directly to his face. In return, Nomed kicks him in the side. They almost send each other flying in opposite directions. Instead, they tumble through the ground.

Nomed gets up, wipes the blood off of his lip and says, "I could have sworn that capsule on your back would have broken by now. Even though I followed your movements I figured your punch would have been weak and feeble, but it actually packed some power behind it. I must admit, I'm impressed."

Norie, who is sitting Indian style on the ground says, "This capsule is unbreakable. I made this out of pure white blood cells and I have hardened them so that this capsule is the strongest element in the world. I did the same to the blood gloves I have on. They are harder than diamonds."

"Let's put that theory to the test," Nomed says, and he dashes towards Norie. The two have a climatic exchange of blows. Neither side giving in to the other. The two clash fists and Nomed realizes that the blood gloves are cracking from the exchange of blows.

Nomed then starts to target those spots while they are exchanging blows and finally, with one big clash, one of Norie's gloves breaks. As soon as it does, Nomed dashes back and springs forward with a punch. Norie turns his last remaining glove into a shield and as he expands it he realized that it has taken major damage and that it won't withstand the punch. Nomed's punch hits the shield and it breaks into pieces. Noire braces himself for the impact of Nomed's blow and is sent flying into the wall.

Nomed says, "So I finally broke through, Norie. Even you must know that even diamonds can be turned into dust."

Norie pulls himself out of the wall and says, "I guess I'll have to make them bigger this time." Norie empties his capsule of blood out of his back and creates the two mallet size gloves again. He bashes them together and says, "Let's try this again."

Nomed says, "There's no way he can swing those things around as easily as he did before. Those things have to weigh a ton. I have to rush him now while my speed is an advantage."

Nomed runs in and dashes behind Norie. He winds back his fist and he thinks to himself, *This is too easy.* In a flash, Norie turns around and smashes Nomed across the face, sending him flying. Nomed's body crashes through a column. As his body hits the ground and rumbles across the ground, he says to himself, *"Damn I felt like that shattered every bone in my body."*
Norie yells to him, "You did it again, Nomed. You rushed in thinking that just because my blood gloves are bigger doesn't mean they weigh more. I've trained for an eon it seems in order to get the strength to wield these things with ease. I am not new to this, Nomed I was born in it."

Meanwhile, Arnoldo leans over to Gillie and says, "Have you seen him take this much damage in a fight before?"

Gillie looks over at him and says, "No and I haven't seen him take this long to find an advantage against an opponent. Rumor is that he is the weakest of the kings so we are going to have a long road ahead of us and I hear these house generals we just defeated are the weakest."
"Do you think he can win this?" Arnoldo asked.
"I've never seen Nomed lose a fight. He always finds a way to win, but I guess we will have to wait and see the outcome of this battle."

A gust of wind flows pass them. They turn back towards the fight they see Nomed and Norie exchanging blows again. Turan walks over and says, "Guys I need you all to stop talking. I'm trying to watch this battle between Gods. Pay attention. He may need us."
Nomed says to himself, "I can't keep this up with him. It's like punching a mountain. Those gloves are strong. I'll have to use my legs as well. His gloves are pretty big. Maybe I could take them out one by one."

Nomed then grabs a hold of one of the gloves at the thumb and jumps on top of the glove. Norie tries to hit him but ends up crashing his glove into the each other.
Norie says, "Don't think I'm going to let you use the fact that my blood gloves are bigger to run around and scamper."

Nomed is still hanging on to the other glove as Norie is shaking it up and down. Norie holds the other glove up and the thumb and pinky fingers turn into blood. The glove engulfs Nomed by the arms and the glove flies off and punches him directly in the stomach. The glove flies into the wall like a rocket, shooting Nomed outside the mansion.

As Nomed's body abruptly hits the ground and goes crashing through the surface, and it creates a crater.

Meanwhile back where Norie and the others are, he turns and looks at them and says, "So now that your leader is out of the way, let's stop this little mutiny and how about you guys just stay here and work for me?"
Shelby walks up and says, "Who do you think we are? Do you really think we are going to join you? We are loyal to Nomed. No one here will be on your side."
Norie says, "Fine. Then all you guys will die here and now."
Immediately, everyone takes their fighting stance because they can feel the killing intent from Norie. He turns his remaining glove into a gun and starts shooting at everyone. Leo grabs his swords and walks in front of everyone, Braden and Turan step up as well. Braden stops the bullets with his mind, Turan burns all the bullets that he could and the remaining bullets Leo slices in half. Gillie then looks at Norie and says, "You're out of blood now, we don't have to worry about you anymore."
Norie begins to laugh and says, "You guys underestimate my power. I don't need blood in my capsule but I will show you what a vampire born of Dracula is capable of. Norie starts to yell. The entire building shakes. As it settles, Norie smiles and says, "Do you guys think that just because you shatter my blood bullets and shields that I can't still use that blood? Let me show you real terror of a blood god."

As everyone looks around. All the chaos caused from the battle of blood on the floor, even the blood that had dried up liquefies and starts going towards Norie. Even the blood stained in everyone's clothes comes out. Nomed looks around in the ground and notices bugs are exploding and birds flying above are exploding. The frogs on the ground are also exploding and the massive blood glove on top of him turns in to liquid and all of it moves towards where Norie is.

Gillie walks up to everyone and says, "He is collecting all of this blood for a reason. If need be I'm ready to move back time if someone dies but we need to formulate a plan on how to avoid it quickly after the first time because I will be out of commission for a while after saving us."

Norie says, "I call pull blood from all over this house, from all of your battles, even the one all the way out by the courts. I'm never out of blood. That's my greatest asset. You guys can't see it but any beast under a certain power level I can make all of the blood come out of their body. It's probably bird feathers and dog and cats laid out around the outsides of this house right now because all of their blood will come to me."

Norie holds up his hand and creates a giant blade. He looks around and says, "Now you will understand why they gave me the name of "Reaper".

As he swing his blade, the sheer force of it breaks through the walls and columns. As it heads for the group, Gillie says, "This should be easy to dodge."

As the giant blood blade comes towards them, they all dodge out of the way, but the pieces of the blade breaks off and follows them, hitting everyone even with them dodging. Shelby screams in pain, and Norie laughs, saying, "Do you guys think you can really run from my blade? I can control it at a whim and make it do my bidding." As he props the giant blade on his shoulder, he says, "I'll make sure that this is the end for you guys."
Braden says, "I think I can stop the momentum of the blade. We just have to worry about the random shard pieces." Norie then swings his sword once more and Turan creates a giant fireball and throws it towards the blade. At the same time, Braden creates a field behind the fireball to keep it from being pushed back. Arnoldo rushes the fireball and punches it to give it momentum. It starts to rattle from the friction.

Meanwhile, Nomed is still in the ground from the crater that his body formed when it hit the ground. He hears Shelby scream and gets infuriated, knowing she is hurt. Nomed tries to get up, but his body won't move. He thinks to himself, *"Is this all the power that I am capable of? I can't protect everyone with this level of powers."*

Then Nomed hears in his head, *"Let loose, stop being afraid of what you are. We won't let you lose control like you did last time."*
Nomed says, "I don't need the power of my father to beat him, I will use my own means."

The voice says, *"This is your power, Nomed. You are your fathers' son. This was passed down to you by him. This is the only way you will win."*

Nomed thinks back to when he first started working for Ms. Gladstone. Back then it was him, Shelby, and Ramon. They practically did everything together and went on missions. They were a perfect family, but one day on a mission, Nomed witnessed Shelby and Ramon about to die and he gave into the darkness. When he regained conciseness and saw bodies and blood all over the place and realized he had killed everyone there. When he looked to see why his right hand wasn't moving, he saw Ramon stopping his arm. Nomed had punched through his chest. After seeing what he had done, Shelby jumped, and she balled up on the floor in terror and looked at Nomed and the horrors he had done.

Nomed panicked and asked himself, "How did this happen?! Shelby told him that his eyes turned black and he went on a rampage."

No matter what the enemy did, his body regenerated and he destroyed them all, but when they were all gone he could differentiate between friend or foe and he attacked them. Ramon protected her from being killed and gave his life in order to get Nomed to regain his consciousness.

As Nomed continues to lay in the ground he says, "I can't unleash that type of power around everyone. I could endanger them again."

The voice says, *"You would rather fight at fifty percent than to save the lives of the ones you claim you love? What a silly vampire you are."*

Nomed yells, "Tell me who you are!"

"I am your father's curse! His bloodline will forever be cursed with an insatiable amount of power so that you can endure anything and have to walk the shadows for all eternity. I am no one, I am nobody, I am nothing; I simply exist. So the question is, are you going to run from the darkness or face it? I haven't been unleashed in 400 years, it would be fun to let loose."

Up in the mansion, the rattling from the blood blade and fireball's force is creating a high pitched squealing noise that almost sounds like a tea pot coming to boil. At the same time, as Leo realized Norie is concentrating on swinging his sword, Leo then unsheathes Shesharuu and the blue dragon goes directly towards Norie. Gillie fires four black bolts towards him as well.

Norie sees what is coming his way and breaks off the back half of the sword while the other part keeps moving forward. With the back half of the sword, he creates a shield that protects him from the bolts and then he slams down Shesharuu with what seems to be blood shackles. With the remaining blood, he throws nails at everyone. As they go ripping through everyone's clothes and body, Norie dashes to the front piece of the sword and kicks it through the fireball. Everybody dodges below it and are hit again. Norie creates a chain as a hilt to make the sword come back to him.

Everyone is laying on the ground in pain as Norie raises his head and says, "Give me my nails back." He rips all of the nails out of people's bodies and creates his giant sword again.

Gillie says, "I'll have to reset time because we won't be able to stop his next attack you guys."

Norie says, "This was entertaining, but I guess I have to kill all of you guys now." As Norie swings his sword and Gillie gets ready to move time back, he sees a red flash come from outside. The flash stops the blade and when the wind settles, everyone sees Nomed stopping the blade with his bare hands.

Turan says, "It's about time you made it back up this way. We were beginning to get a little worried and beat up."

Shelby chimes in, "Guys, we need to be worried if Nomed has given into the darkness."

Everyone looks at Shelby and says, "What do you mean? He seems fine."

Shelby shudders in terror and says, "Look into his eyes. They are all black. Last time he did this, he killed one of his teammates."

Gillie turns around and says, "That's why you guys never bring up the reason I was bought onto the team."

Shelby says regrettably, "With that being said I need everyone to be ready to take him down if he wins this battle."

Nomed then looks back at them and says, "You guys have nothing to worry about, but truthfully she is right. If I lose control you need to kill me, but it is taking everything in me not to lose it, so I apologize now for not talking. It's just best I stay silent and keep my composure."

Nomed then breaks Norie's sword in half and rushes towards him and punches at him. Norie puts up a shield and is knocked back from the remarkable force of the punch.

"You really are your father's son. I haven't seen eyes like that in a long time. How does the demon rage feel? Powerful right? But you are still no match for me."

Nomed just continues to stare at Norie as Norie says, "You're not even the same smart mouth punk that walked in here. I see you are finally taking this serious."

Nomed rushes in and kicks at Norie into a column. Norie then creates a giant foot and kicks Nomed the other way. By the time Norie gets up from the ground, Nomed is already running towards him. As he creates his huge blood gloves again he swings to hit Nomed, who easily slams it to the ground and begins to land multiple punches against Norie's body.

Norie puts up a shield between the two of them and at the same time catches Nomed's hands in the blood shield. From the shield, he creates dozen of little fists that begin to deliver the same pain Nomed was dishing out. As the punches continue, Nomed lets out a yell and breaks himself free. Norie then kicks Nomed across the room.

Norie says to himself, *"No one can break that out of sheer strength. I need to hurry up and end this before he taps into more of his demon rage. If he becomes anything like his father he will kill me in no time."*

Norie then looks over to Nomed's group and says, "I will target them and then wait for an opening to kill Nomed." Norie then creates his giant sword once more and swings it towards Nomed's crew.

Nomed makes it in front of the blade in seconds and as he holds the blade he feels this sensation. Nomed thinks back and says to himself, *"When have I felt this?"* and he remembers the plane ride to Atlantis. That moment was where Norie pulled a blood knife on him and he felt as if he had seen or used that power before. It felt very familiar. As the force of the blade is driving Nomed back, the blade begins to rumble in his hand uncontrollably. Even Norie notices it and says, "What the hell is going on here?!" Nomed hears the voice again. It says, *"Take this power. Everything gifted can be returned to its owner. Now that you have it, use over your inner power. You can use this!!"*
Nomed looks down and says, "It's just a blade," the voice then says, *"No, Nomed! Really look at it."*

Nomed actually takes time to look now and notices by looking hard enough he can actually see the blood moving in working inside the blade. The voice says, *"Now take what is rightfully yours."* Nomed then let's his hands off of the blade. When it hits his body, it turns into blood.

Calderon says, "What he fuck did I just witness?"

He then taps Turan and says, "Did you see that shit?" Then he looks at Braden and before he can ask Braden says, "Yes I saw it. Nomed then holds up his hands and half of the sword turns into blood. As Norie lifts up the other half his face is in shock. He says, "I can't believe you actually have the ability to use powers that were handed down by your father. Only one person should be able to do that and that's him. Not you, not some untrained rookie that has no idea how to handle his own power."

Nomed says, "Well I am his son. Why would you think I wouldn't be able to? You should know better than me that traits are passed from father to son."

"I have to end this now," Norie says, and with all of the blood that's on the floor Norie creates arrows with them and throws them at Nomed, who continues to dodge and dance around them.

As they all hit the ground, Nomed asks, "Is that the best you have to offer?" In the same sentence, the arrows in the ground change around to where the arrow is not the ground anymore it is pointed at Nomed.

They then launch at him and he moves most of them out of the way, but several hit his legs and arms and even his back. Nomed hunches over and you can see the blood dripping from his wounds, Norie notices it as well and creates two swords that charge at Nomed.

"You won't be able to dodge as well with your movement restricted," Norie says.

Norie starts to slash and swing at Nomed, who is dodging his attacks and suddenly his leg gives out and he is forced to jump out of the way. As he lands, he grimaces in pain. Norie smiles and rushed towards Nomed again but before he reaches him, Nomed dashes past him.

As Norie turns his head to see Nomed on one knee with a clear sword in his hand, Norie looks down and realizes his body as almost been sliced in half. Nomed looks Norie in the eye, turns the sword towards him and extends it through his chest.

Nomed gets up and brushes off the arrows and begins to walk normally again, as Norie says, "I thought the arrows hit you, I saw you bleeding."

Nomed says, "You thought you saw me bleeding. Now that I have the power of blood manipulation all I did was make the sharpest part of the arrows drip blood and concentrate on the arrows to make it seem like I was injured, which you fell for. Once you saw that I was weakened, you charged in like a hungry wolf looking to take a bite out of me, not paying attention to the details of the arrows or even the mere fact that I was actually dodging your attacks. When we first started this battle you said I was underestimating you and that I didn't know the extent of your powers. I wasn't just rushing you I was learning your powers that you so boastfully showed and explained each time after you used them, and when I gained your power I already had knowledge of how to use them.

Your major flaw was that you're so use to carrying your capsule around you never even noticed I took your white blood cell capsule off your back. You have gotten accustomed to how light it is on your back after carrying it for so long. As you said, it is the hardest material in the world, so why wouldn't I try to use it against you? You said I wasn't worthy of being a vampire king and that I didn't pay attention to detail and that I was too young, but I have shown you that as much as you did not believe it you were the fool and the weak one. All of this hiding and staying in this mansion has made you weak and you have forgotten what it feels like to be in the midst of a real battle and how when the little things change around you, how you should notice them and change along with the circumstances. My father would be disappointed in you if he was to see how far you have fallen from being a true king."

Norie says, "Do you think the others will idly stand by after hearing what happened? Here I am, the weakest of the three, you won't stand a chance against the others. I will rejoice when they kill you, but the day I'm lectured by some snot nose punk and at the moment Nomed cuts his head off of his body and says, "I guess you don't have to listen anymore then."

"King"

Nomed turns and looks at all of his friends, as his eyes go from jet black back to their normal red glowing color and he says he has now completed the first step.

Nomed walks to Norie's throne and sits down. He pulls a little capsule of blood out of the metal canteen along with the ring with everyone else's blood in it and says, "This is Anima's blood and yours," as he forges a brilliant ring that he puts around the necklace he had on his neck. As he crushes the ring that was made from their blood.

Nomed continues on, "You guys have all proved your loyalty to me and at this time I give anyone of you the right to leave if you felt this battle was too much. Does anyone want to leave?"

Braden steps forward and says, "No Nomed, we are here with you until we all meet our doom or share the glory of you being king." "Well share a toast with me," Nomed says as he creates a blood challis. "Drink a sip of Norie's blood. The demon rage inside of me told me that just a sip of his blood could allow you to gain a new power and this is a power that we will all need for the battles ahead of us. At this time, we must get stronger."

Everyone takes a sip as they continue to listen to Nomed speak, "With that being said I must pick a first and second in command. First will be Braden and second will be Gillie. Arnoldo you will be my head in training. I hope that's not too big of a task for you."

Shelby walks forward and says, "I guess you are about to go to sleep again. Try to wake up faster this time just in case we need you." Nomed smiles and says, "Hopefully by then you guys have grown some and turned this place into our home."

Nomed then sternly looks at Braden and Gillie and says, "One person at my side at all times."

Nomed then drops the challis and passes out. As the challis rolls on the ground, it turns to liquid with everyone looking at it.

…..TO BE CONTINUED

www.ingramcontent.com/pod-product-compliance
Lightning Source LLC
Chambersburg PA
CBHW041406010726
47507CB00001B/14